As soon as she sat down, Jessica heard a nasty, high-pitched titter. After a moment a couple of other voices chimed in. A cold feeling of dread seeped through Jessica's skin.

Trying not to cue anyone in to how self-conscious she felt, Jessica casually glanced around. Out of the corner of her eye she caught sight of an El Carro girl leaning over to whisper to a friend.

What was going on? Jessica started to panic. Was there toilet paper stuck to her shoe or something? Had someone slapped a Kick Me sign on her back? Frantically she looked down at herself, scanning for anything that was torn, stained, or unbuttoned.

Then she saw it—and almost screamed.

For a moment she couldn't move or breathe. It was as if she'd had the wind knocked out of her.

Written across the top of the blackboard in big, jagged, white letters were the words *Jessica Wakefield is a slut.*

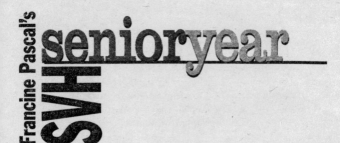

Francine Pascal's SVH senioryear

Say It to My Face

CREATED BY
FRANCINE PASCAL

BANTAM BOOKS
NEW YORK • TORONTO • LONDON • SYDNEY • AUCKLAND

RL 6, age 12 and up

SAY IT TO MY FACE
A Bantam Book / March 1999

Sweet Valley High® is a registered trademark of Francine Pascal.
Conceived by Francine Pascal.
Cover photography by Michael Segal.

Produced by 17th Street Productions,
a division of Daniel Weiss Associates, Inc.
33 West 17th Street
New York, NY 10011.

ISBN: 0-553-57027-7

Published simultaneously in the United States and Canada

Bantam Books are published by Bantam Books, a division of Random
House, Inc. Its trademark, consisting of the words "Bantam Books" and
the portrayal of a rooster, is Registered in U.S. Patent and Trademark
Office and in other countries. Marca Registrada. Bantam Books, 1540
Broadway, New York, New York 10036.

PRINTED IN THE UNITED STATES OF AMERICA

OPM   0 9 8 7 6 5 4 3 2 1

To Molly Jessica W. Wenk

Jessica Wakefield

I used to think that love was about losing yourself. Letting yourself go and letting the person you loved be there to catch you. The thing is, the guys I pick never seem to be willing to play catcher. They always just sort of want to play, I don't know, Ping-Pong or something.

Elizabeth Wakefield

Love is about trust. It's about opening yourself up to a person and knowing that he'll respect the fact that you're baring your soul. It's about sharing. Being totally equal in a relationship and not losing a sense of who you are just to please the other person. I truly believe that old saying that you have to love yourself before you can really love someone else. Because when you're in love, holding on to your sense of self can be difficult. But the more aware you are of <u>who</u> you are, the less likely you are to let someone . . . I'm repeating myself, aren't I?

Here's one thing I know for sure. Crushes are not love. They're temporary, fleeting, and often totally unfounded. Do not mistake a crush for love. Unless you want your <u>heart</u> crushed.

Conner McDermott

Love stinks.

Maria Slater

I've never been in love. At least, I don't
<u>think</u> I have. I guess if I were, I would've
known it, though, right?

I'm looking forward to that bolt of lightning.
It sounds improbable, but it would be great if it
actually happened.

Melissa Fox

Love is always being there for each other. Helping each other through your mistakes. Unconditional love.

And forgiveness.

If you want love to last, you have to practice forgiveness—even in the most painful situations. If you don't think you can do that, don't even bother. Because contrary to the male population's widespread belief, none of them are perfect.

Not one.

Not even Will.

CHAPTER
Hard to Hate

1

"What *the hell* are you doing here?" Conner McDermott shouted.

Elizabeth Wakefield squeezed her eyes shut. *This is a dream—a bizarrely vivid nightmare—and when I open my eyes, he'll be gone.*

She did, and he wasn't. Conner McDermott, *the* Conner McDermott, was standing in front of her, wearing nothing but a towel around his waist. Elizabeth had to remind herself to breathe.

"I'm—I'm sorry," she stammered, sucking air. "I need . . . uh, I need . . ."

She trailed off, unable to formulate a coherent sentence. Conner had been the focus of every one of her daydreams for the past few days, but she had never imagined him quite like this—beads of water dripping from his dark hair onto his glistening shoulders. Quite a jolt to the heart for a Sunday morning.

"So you're the helpless little waif my sister brought home." Conner's green eyes were piercing. "Shacking up with Barbie. I can't believe it.

Don't you have some pink Malibu Dream House you can run off to or something?"

"Wait . . . your sister?" she sputtered, wrenching her gaze from Conner's six-pack abs.

"I know you're not a rocket scientist, but . . . my half sister? Megan Sandborn?" Conner prompted impatiently.

Sister? But their last names were—oh. That was the *half* part.

"Okay," Elizabeth said hastily. She touched her hand to her forehead. "Yeah, Megan said I could stay here until my house was rebuilt. We work together on the *Oracle*." Good. She was making sense now.

"Oh, right, the school paper." Conner's voice seethed with sarcasm. "What do you cover, hard-hitting news stories like whether the cafeteria should serve regular milk *and* chocolate milk?"

"Well, at least I do something instead of just ranking on everything!" Elizabeth's embarrassment was turning to indignation. What right did he have to take an attitude with her? "What activities are *you* involved in—president of the Little Ironic Remarks club?"

Conner smirked. "I think we have an opening for treasurer. Interested?"

She stared up at him, too infuriated to speak. For a moment his eyes locked with hers. Feeling totally self-conscious, Elizabeth looked down . . .

2

then realized she was staring at his chest again. She focused on the tile wall above his head.

"I . . ." She came up with nothing. Damn, he was annoying.

From the moment she first encountered Conner in her creative-writing class, Elizabeth had known that he wasn't someone she would ever even hang out with. He was the kind of jaded-and-disheveled cynic who felt the compulsive need to tear everything down because he thought it made him look cool. He'd made that pretty clear on the first day of creative-writing class. Elizabeth had been explaining her reasons for taking the class when Conner had introduced himself by laughing at her, then harshing on her comments.

The fact that he'd read her essay aloud with a voice like an angel's, practically bringing tears to Elizabeth's eyes, hadn't swayed her opinion one iota. Not one.

She was *so* not the kind of ditzy girl who went after those Kurt Cobain–wanna-be types. She wasn't interested in playing mother figure to some slacker who was probably going to end up in a Zeppelin tribute band playing weddings.

So why was she still standing frozen in the middle of a steamy bathroom with Conner?

"You are one of the most obnoxious people I've ever met," Elizabeth spat after a long at-a-loss pause.

"Thanks for sharing." Conner suppressed the urge to let his furious glare splinter into laughter. It was just too easy to get a rise out of Elizabeth.

He was beyond pissed that she was apparently staying in his house—but it was actually kind of funny to see how ridiculously embarrassed she was at the moment. Way more embarrassed than a normal person walking in on somebody in a towel. A normal person would have left five minutes ago.

Elizabeth was gripping the doorknob so hard, her knuckles were white.

"You know, you could get over yourself long enough to be a little civil," she went on, her voice gaining strength. "I didn't ask to have my house totaled and have nowhere else to go."

Conner tried hard not to notice the way her blue-green eyes were flashing or the hollow of collarbone heaving just above the V neck of her T-shirt.

Oh, man. He couldn't believe he was going to have to navigate the minefield of having Elizabeth Wakefield in his own house. She was the first girl he'd ever met who surprised him—who busted all the stereotypes wide open. And that meant he could never let himself get close to her. Conner knew when to close himself off to disappointment and hurt. He'd practically turned it into an art form. But just the effort of not finding Elizabeth attractive was making the hairs on the back of his neck stand up. Then again, maybe that was just the cold air rushing into the steam-filled bathroom.

"Point taken," Conner said curtly. "Well, it was lovely running into you. Now would you mind getting the hell out of here so I can shave in peace?"

"Gladly," Elizabeth shot back. She swept from the room in a swirl of steam, leaving the door open behind her.

Conner stepped out of the shower and slammed the door shut, a little harder than was necessary. *This is all I need right now,* he thought grimly, rubbing the bathroom mirror to clear the condensation away.

Conner stared at his reflection as he gripped the sides of the sink. This was totally not cool. He worked so hard to draw a line between his family life and his school life. And now the one person who he had already sworn he'd never let into his world had been *invited* in by his own sister. Barbie was going to have to go.

"Conner!"

The door connecting his room to the bathroom was flung open and Megan was standing there, looking all accusatory.

"God, Sandy! This was still *my* bathroom the last time I checked!"

"Yeah, well, it's not anymore," Megan said. She was holding on to the damn doorknob just like Elizabeth had. "You have to share it with Elizabeth now. Why were you yelling at her?"

"She walked in on me," Conner said. "Not unlike someone else I know. What is it with you people?"

"You people?" Megan's eyebrows shot up.

"Girls!" Conner said, reaching up to wipe off the mirror again. "You think you own the whole world."

Megan rolled her eyes. "You sound like a five-year-old, Conner."

"Thanks, Sandy," he spat. "She's not staying."

"Why? Do you have a problem with Elizabeth?" Megan asked.

Conner snorted. "Where do I start?"

Actually, it was a thorny question. Where *should* he start? Not with the deeply affecting essay that had forced him to admit Elizabeth Wakefield was more than just a vapid blonde. Not with the dance he'd skipped in order to avoid her. Definitely not with how sexy she looked when her heart-shaped face flared pink with embarrassment and anger.

"You know what? Forget it," Conner said finally. He bowed his head slightly and stared at the drain, defeated. "Will you just get out of here?"

"Whatever," Megan said. She glanced at the ceiling imploringly, as if asking for answers about her brother's insanity.

Once the door was closed, Conner blew out a heavy sigh of exasperation.

It wasn't Megan's fault he had some weird vibes going with Elizabeth. She had been so excited to bond with someone at her new school. Losing El

6

Carro High in the quake wasn't that big a deal to him, but Megan had spent the summer haunted by the fear that she wouldn't make any friends at Sweet Valley High. For her an extended slumber party with Elizabeth was just what the doctor ordered.

He didn't have the heart to take that away from her, as unthinkable as the alternative was.

"This sucks," Conner said, lifting his head to glower at his reflection.

He suddenly felt even more caged in than usual. Elizabeth was going to be in his face 24/7. How would he keep his secrets to himself? What went on in his life was nobody's business.

He glanced at the door that connected to her bedroom. And why did she have to be so damn hot?

Jessica Wakefield placed a carton of skim milk on her tray and slid it along the cafeteria line. Monday was greasy pizza day, and she could practically feel the zits forming on her face. Why didn't they just serve pork rinds dipped in lard and sprinkled with bacon bits?

But it didn't really matter what they were offering anyway. Jessica was too nervous to eat. She was anticipating a confrontation, and that was never good for her digestive system.

Jessica unenthusiastically selected a large salad and a yogurt. Not exactly mouthwatering, but good energy foods for pretryout cheerleading practice. She could attempt to get them down. As she headed toward the checkout counter, she heard a familiar laugh and froze. Casually Jessica looked up. Melissa Fox was coming toward her, flanked by her friends Cherie Reese and Gina Cho.

It was strange how Melissa could be so pretty when her features were so angular, her eyes so piercing. Melissa's face didn't register surprise or anger at the sight of Jessica. Instead her eyes locked on Jessica's face, unflinching. She let her gaze flicker down to the vinyl miniskirt Jessica had borrowed from Lila's closet that morning.

This was it. Jessica's shoulders tightened. *You didn't know Will had a girlfriend,* she reminded herself. *And when you found out, you broke it off with him. You didn't do anything wrong.* So why were her palms sweating? Jessica took a deep breath and steeled herself for whatever Melissa was going to say.

Melissa lowered her chin and whispered something in Cherie's direction, never taking her ice blue eyes off Jessica.

Cherie tilted her head back and snorted. Then she loudly stage-whispered, "Oh, I'm sorry, are we in a sleazy nightclub? Silly me, I thought this was the cafeteria."

Gina burst out laughing. Melissa's thin lips flattened into a smile, but her eyes were narrowed and unchanging.

Jessica opened her mouth, ready to retort—something along the lines of, "Is that the best you can do?" Then she saw him. Will was standing a few paces behind Melissa, his hands at his sides, looking as if he wasn't sure whether to come closer.

As Jessica's words died in her mouth, Will met her eye. His blue-eyed gaze was pained—apologetic or embarrassed—she couldn't tell.

Either way, just looking at him hurt. How could he just stand there, letting her take their abuse, knowing *he* had caused all this?

Melissa breezed past her. Jessica realized a second too late that she had let them get the last word. Will hesitated, and for a sickeningly nerve-racking moment Jessica thought he was about to come over to her. Then he followed Melissa, swerving to keep his distance from Jessica.

Irrational tears stung Jessica's eyes. She stared down at the floor, trying hard to blot out the memory of the intense yet tender way Will Simmons had kissed her. *There was no deep connection,* she reminded herself bitterly. Will was just using her, trying to sneak a quickie on the side before he slunk back to his girlfriend like the dog he was. The problem was, Will had seemed so sweet and so different from other guys. But he was just a fake, and not worth her tears.

Jessica blinked a few times and quickly glanced down at her skirt. After Cherie's comment it suddenly felt six inches shorter than it was. She could just skip lunch and go home to change her clothes. But that would mean conceding defeat, and that was not something Jessica was willing to do.

Jessica lifted her chin and started weaving through the cafeteria toward her friends' table. Maybe Melissa and Will had been Mr. and Ms. Popularity at El Carro, but this was Jessica's school. There was nothing they could do to her here. If Melissa wanted to be petty, that was fine. Jessica was ready for anything Melissa was going to bring her way. She could hold her own.

Hopefully. Maybe.

Jessica Wakefield

People always say you shouldn't judge a book by its cover. But come on, everyone does it. I know I do. I really think that anybody who says they don't judge people on first impressions is a big liar.

So, lately I've been wondering how people see me when they meet me. For practically the first time in my life, my high school isn't filled with people who've known me since my idea of stimulating entertainment was eating Play-Doh.

I've always been popular. And my image has always been important to me because I know how important first impressions are. But when people meet me, do they see me as a cool person . . . or do they just see me as this dumb blonde who's popular because she follows the crowd?

I feel like I spend all this time and energy putting myself together because it really matters to me that people like me. But then sometimes I just let my emotions take over, and I end up undoing all my hard work.

Like with Will. I really liked him. Before I actually knew anything about him. And when I found out he had a girlfriend, I got so upset, I totally went off . . . without thinking for a second about how I would sound or who might be listening. And now the first impression I made to the most popular girl at ECH is that I'm an evil, home-wrecking bitch.

This may be one problem good hair and a fab outfit won't fix.

Maria Slater brushed some lint particles off the knees of her green army pants as she made her way out of the SVH auditorium on Monday afternoon. Why did drama class always include cringe-worthy acting exercises that involved "interpreting" random words like *molten* and *amoeba*? And why did those so-called interpretations inevitably consist of crawling around on a dusty stage floor?

She wondered if it was too soon to consider dropping the class. But she'd promised herself she would get back into drama this year. If nothing else, it would hone her acting ability just to maintain a serious expression while watching Aaron Dallas writhe across the floorboards re-creating *turgid*.

Maria glanced at her watch. Drama had let out a few minutes early, so she could probably catch Elizabeth on her way out of creative writing. Maria hadn't seen much of her best friend since school started, except at *Oracle* meetings. But Elizabeth's life was pretty hectic these days, with her moving into that girl Megan's house. Plus the last time Elizabeth called, Maria had been busy working on her college applications.

I guess that's what I get for being the queen of the geeks, Maria reflected as the clopping of her wooden-soled clogs echoed across the cinder-block walls of the empty corridor. She'd been so stressed out about school and college applications that she hadn't really had time to think about anything else.

With each grueling hour she spent working on her early-decision application for Yale, Maria felt more like she was living in an exhausting, depressing parallel universe. Everyone around her talked about senior year as their big chance to let loose, go wild, and blow off everything related to academics. But every quiz, every paper, every extracurricular activity might mean the difference between getting an edge over the competition or spending the rest of her life asking, "Do you want fries with that?" It boggled her mind that nobody else seemed to have any concept of their future beyond senior skip day.

The final bell of the period rang. All around Maria crowds of students erupted from doorways, chattering and laughing as they headed down the hallway. She scanned the sea of faces—so many new people she hadn't met yet. The El Carro kids had only been around for a week, and everyone already seemed to be part of a group or a couple. Everyone except Maria.

Even though she was constantly putting on a

school-spirit front, sometimes Maria wished the El Carro kids would all just go back where they came from. It was so much easier to not feel lonely when she at least recognized everybody.

But it wasn't their fault they were here. Not their fault their school—and maybe their homes and friends and families—had been lost in the quake. Maria couldn't believe she was being so uncharitable.

Maybe she was insane to let her life revolve around school. After all, everything she had worked for could be reduced to rubble in seconds. Maybe she should spend more of her senior year hanging out and meeting people—acting like a normal, socially functioning human being.

Maria stationed herself off to the side of Elizabeth's classroom and someone passing through caught her eye. In fact, "caught" was an understatement—"demanded" was more like it. Conner McDermott, one of the new ECH seniors and possibly the hottest guy she had ever seen in her life, was walking right toward her.

Why did I never bother to figure out how to look cool at moments like this? Maria wondered. Conner had lost the ratty old overcoat he'd been wearing the last time Maria had seen him. Now he had on a white V-neck T-shirt that clung to his chest in all the right places. His head bent slightly as he walked, and it occurred to Maria that it didn't matter how uncool she was. He wouldn't notice her if she were standing in the middle of the hallway wearing a string bikini.

Luckily that gave her all the more time to stare without getting caught. Unluckily the moment she realized this, he looked up.

Snagged, Maria thought. But instead of getting all flustered, she ventured a tiny smile. He lifted his eyebrows and turned up the corners of his lips noncommittally. Then he passed right by her. Maria willed her eyes to look away. "Gaping idiot" was not the impression she wanted to make.

Maria felt her timid smile bloom into a silly little grin. So he hadn't exactly swept her off her feet and promised to take her away from all this. But he had noticed her. That was interesting.

Maybe she really *should* make an effort to get to know some of the new seniors.

Elizabeth rose from her desk in slow motion as she watched Conner quickly slip out of the room. As far as she was concerned, he couldn't get away fast enough. Maybe now she could regain control over her thought process.

Glancing down at the blank page in her notebook, Elizabeth realized she'd barely heard Mr. Quigley give out the assignment. She thought they were supposed to write a two-page character study, but for all she really knew, it could have been an epic poem about circus clowns.

With a slight groan Elizabeth shuffled slowly toward the door so it wouldn't look like she was trying to catch up with Conner.

Making a point of not following him out is just as bad as following him out, a nagging little voice taunted her. *Either way, you're spending way too much mental energy on this guy.*

She still couldn't believe the irony of her situation. Just when she'd realized she had an immense, unhealthy crush on a guy who was totally wrong for her and just when she'd promised herself to stop thinking about him and focus on other things, she ended up being his new roomie. Fate had a sick sense of humor.

"Liz?" Enid Rollins said as she got up from her desk near the door. "I'm going to have to cancel on our mall spree tonight. Ileana and I are getting together to work on some ideas for a new 'zine."

"No problem," Elizabeth said quickly. She had no recollection of making shopping plans with Enid. It seemed her brain malfunctions were increasing.

"Good. I'll catch you later!" Enid said before disappearing into the crowded hallway.

Elizabeth didn't bother to answer. She and Enid had been best friends for a long time, but lately they never seemed to be able to coordinate their schedules.

"Liz! Over here!"

Elizabeth turned and saw Maria waiting near

the wall. She looked nonchalantly gorgeous as usual, in a crocheted top Elizabeth could never have pulled off.

"God, are you on another planet today?" Maria grinned as she fell into step beside Elizabeth. "Didn't you hear me? I felt like an idiot standing there calling you."

"Sorry," Elizabeth said, a little hoarsely. "I guess I'm just out of it. I didn't sleep too well last night. You know, strange bed and all that." Not to mention a strange guy sleeping down the hall from her.

"I know what you mean. But this'll wake you up. You know that hottie we were talking about the other day, Conner McDermott?" Maria pointed. Elizabeth glimpsed Conner's back disappearing down the hall. "I just saw him coming out of your class, and he totally checked me out!"

Elizabeth felt her throat constrict. "Oh, wow."

Maria shook her head admiringly in Conner's direction. "I can't believe you don't think he's cute, Liz. He is, like, a breathtaking specimen."

"Yeah, well, he's . . . not really my type," Elizabeth said carefully.

"True. He's not exactly that all-American jock stud you usually go for." Maria giggled. "But maybe he's not as antisocial as he seemed at first. Have you ever talked to him?"

"Uh . . . yeah, actually." The image of Conner's broad chest, covered by nothing more than a glistening

18

sheen of water, popped into Elizabeth's mind She felt like the temperature in the hallway had just gone up about ten degrees.

"You have?" Maria turned to look at Elizabeth, her face bright with surprise. "So, spill! What's he like? What happened?"

Elizabeth hesitated. *I found him half naked in my shower? Nah.* Suddenly telling Maria that she and Conner lived in the same house seemed like a bad idea. Maria would make a huge deal out of it, and Elizabeth wanted to avoid the subject as much as possible. It was bad enough that her own mind kept bringing him up without warning—she didn't need Maria doing it too. But Maria was going to find out eventually.

"Actually, he's, uh, he's Megan's brother," Elizabeth said, trying to keep her voice light. "Well, half brother. But I've talked to him at the house."

Maria stopped in her tracks and held up her palm to Elizabeth. "Hold up. Rewind." Her eyes were wide. "Are you telling me you actually *live* with this guy?"

"Um, yeah. Can we drop it now?" Without waiting for an answer, Elizabeth maneuvered around a huge group of freshmen and took off down the hall. Maria kept up.

"Get *out!*" Maria exclaimed, giving Elizabeth's shoulder a playful shove. "You go, Liz! That is too cool." Maria shook her head, a wicked grin on her face. "Now I understand why you left Lila's big old mansion to go stay at Megan's! Omigod. Have you, like, seen him in his underwear? C'mon, Liz, boxers or briefs?"

"No! I mean, I don't know!" Elizabeth said, a little too quickly. "I already told you, Maria, he is not my type."

"Cool. Then when I come over, you can introduce us and strategically retreat to your room, right?"

Elizabeth felt an irrational surge of possessiveness. Her jaw tightened.

"You really wouldn't even like him if you met him, Maria," Elizabeth said, amazed that she sounded so calm. "He's a total pig."

"A pig," Maria repeated.

"Yeah. I mean, his room is a mess. It just reeks, and he, uh, doesn't clean up after himself. . . ." *And he's really smart and loves his sister and looks incredible shirtless.* "He's just not boyfriend material," Elizabeth finished lamely.

"Hmmm. So you don't like him because he's hygienically challenged." Maria's tone was half perplexed, half amused. "I'd have to rule out dating the entire male population based on that assessment. However, given that Conner is possibly the hottest guy I've ever encountered, I think I'll take my chances. I just won't take him anywhere he might use the wrong fork or something."

Take him somewhere? Maria and Conner on a date? That could never happen.

"So, do you feel like coming over to study tonight?" Maria said. "Or *I* could come over to *your* place." She looked just a tad too psyched about that prospect.

At that moment Elizabeth wanted nothing less than to see Maria and Conner in the same room. "Um, can I let you know? I've kind of got a lot going on right now," Elizabeth hedged.

"Okay. Just give me a call later," Maria said as the bell rang. She started walking backward down the hall. "But don't be thinking you're going to keep that boy all to yourself!" she called.

Elizabeth hugged her notebook to her chest. What if she *wanted* to keep Conner to herself?

Jessica was so ready for this day to be over. Ever since her close encounter with Melissa and her entourage at lunch, she'd felt like every guy in school was leering at her legs and every girl was sneering at them. *Only two more classes to go,* she thought as she walked through the hall. In a couple of hours she would go home, strip off Lila's vinyl miniskirt, and stuff it back in her walk-in closet where it belonged.

Jessica turned the corner and saw a couple of El Carro girls she recognized from cheerleading. She acknowledged them with a distracted nod. As they passed by, Jessica heard a burst of laughter behind her. She whirled around and saw the two girls walking with their heads bent together. One of them craned her neck to glance back over her shoulder, but when she spotted Jessica looking, she quickly faced forward and let out another burst of giggles.

"Can you even *believe* that outfit?" one girl not so subtly whispered.

"Melissa was right," the other answered before walking into a classroom. "Who does she think she is?"

Jessica felt a little weak in the knees but forced herself to keep walking, pretending not to notice. Had Melissa and her friends put out an all-points bulletin with the fashion police? Maybe she should get her gym bag and change into her sweats. Jessica glanced up at the hall clock. There was no time. And it was a ridiculous idea anyway. The day was almost over.

She picked up her pace, even though she wasn't exactly psyched to get to her math class. Everyone she knew and hated would be present and accounted for.

"Jessica."

She stopped short. The sound of his voice caused her skin to tingle. Jessica turned around, adopting a disinterested expression.

"What do you want, Will?" she asked with more malice in her tone than she actually felt. She wanted to feel malice. She really did.

Will took a tentative step closer. "I just wanted

you to know that . . . well, that—" Will looked up, past her shoulder, and backed up again. Jessica glanced behind her and watched Gina slip into her classroom.

"What, Will?" Jessica asked, feeling sure that he was going to turn and bolt now that he'd been caught in the act of talking to her.

"I have to go," he said quietly, looking at the floor. "Sorry."

His broad back hunched slightly as he retreated down the hall. "Me too," Jessica whispered. She looked at her classroom door. "Because now I'm sure Gina is in there telling your girlfriend what she saw and Melissa is getting ready to tear my eyes out."

Jessica walked into the classroom, feeling like an open target. She slipped into her usual seat by the door, pointedly keeping her eyes from the back of the room, where Melissa, Cherie, Gina, and half the football team always camped out.

As soon as she sat down, Jessica heard a nasty, high-pitched titter. After a moment a couple of other voices chimed in. A cold feeling of dread seeped through Jessica's skin.

Trying not to cue anyone in to how self-conscious she felt, Jessica casually glanced around. Out of the corner of her eye she caught sight of an El Carro girl leaning over to whisper to a friend.

What was going on? Jessica started to panic.

23

Was there toilet paper stuck to her shoe or something? Had someone slapped a Kick Me sign on her back? Frantically she looked down at herself, scanning for anything that was torn, stained, or unbuttoned.

Then she saw it—and almost screamed.

For a moment she couldn't move or breathe. It was as if she'd had the wind knocked out of her.

Written across the top of the blackboard in big, jagged, white letters were the words *Jessica Wakefield is a slut*.

Jessica stood up slowly and walked on shaky legs toward the door, a loud chorus of laughter following her. Once she hit the deserted hallway, she started to sprint.

"Jess!" Lila's voice called after her, but it was nearly drowned out by the sound of the blood rushing through Jessica's ears. She bashed open the heavy wooden door to the bathroom with the heels of her hands, jolting her arms painfully. She didn't care. How could anyone do such a thing? Jessica had never heard of anything so blatantly vicious in her life.

"Jessica, are you okay?" Lila stood next to Jessica, one hand nervously playing with the fingers of the other, as if she was afraid to touch her friend.

"Who—who—would—" Jessica held her stomach and tried not to double over as she cried.

Lila put an arm around Jessica's shoulders and

pulled a paper towel from the metal dispenser on the wall. Jessica took it from her and pressed the coarse paper against her face. She couldn't get the image of that jagged scrawl out of her mind.

"I don't know who did it, Jess, but I'm sure Mr. Schneider's reaming everybody out right now," Lila said. Jessica hoisted herself up onto the low windowsill, grateful that the window was made of thick, cloudy glass. She took a deep breath as her tears slowed.

"God, Li," Jessica said, her voice a meek quaver. "Everyone hates me." She knew she sounded irrational, but she felt hopeless. No one had ever been so mean to her. Never.

"No, they don't," Lila said. She tugged on Jessica's wrist. "Come on. Let's fix your face and go back to class."

Jessica's eyes filled with hot tears once again. She stared at the blotched paper towel in her hand. "You go," she said, staring at the opaque window. "I think I'll stay here for a while."

"It'll be okay," Lila said in a confident voice.

"Yeah," Jessica whispered as Lila backed toward the door. "Sure, it will."

The bell rang, and Jessica rushed to Ms. Dalton's classroom. Her back hurt from spending the last forty minutes curled against the bathroom window, crying, and she was pretty sure she had permanent lines indented in her thighs from the edge of the windowsill. Waiting for the bell to ring, Jessica had worked herself into a state of heightened agitation. Nothing like this had ever happened to her before, and she had no idea how to react, although the crying part had seemed to come rather naturally. She needed to talk to Elizabeth. Luckily eighth-period French was the only class they had together.

Jessica rushed up behind Elizabeth and grabbed her sister's arm before she could walk into the classroom.

"Liz!"

"Ow, Jess!" Elizabeth complained as Jessica dragged her down the hallway. She wrested her arm out of Jessica's grip. "What are you *doing?*"

"You're never going to believe what happened to me," Jessica whispered, the tears starting to well up all over again. "I sat down in math and someone had written 'Jessica is a slut' on the blackboard."

Elizabeth's hand flew to her mouth. "Oh, Jess!"

"Tell me the truth," Jessica said, blinking rapidly as she wrapped her arms protectively around her waist. "Have you heard anything? What are people saying about me?" Jessica loathed the hysterical note in her voice.

"I haven't heard anything," Elizabeth said, gently pulling Jessica toward the wall and away from the crowd. She searched Jessica's face. "Are you going to be okay?"

26

"I can't believe Will would do this to me," Jessica said, feeling the weight of his cruelty pressing against her chest. "He used *me*. He led *me* on. All I did was kiss him."

That wasn't all she'd done, not really. She'd cared about him. Allowed herself to hope for something real. She'd even said *we*. Out loud. To him.

"And now he's spreading rumors about me! He must be telling people that we . . . that we—" Jessica's eyes burned. "Liz, why would he go so far out of his way to torture me?"

A stray tear snaked down Jessica's cheek, and she angrily wiped it away. She had to stop feeling so wounded and concentrate on being angry. She'd shed enough tears over Will.

"Who knows why guys do anything?" Elizabeth said. "But all your friends know you're not like that. Whatever Will or Melissa says about you, I'm sure nobody will really believe it—"

"Why wouldn't they?" Jessica didn't realize she had raised her voice until she noticed a passing El Carro girl turn to her friend and roll her eyes. The friend laughed. "Will and Melissa are really popular," Jessica added quietly. "God only knows what disgusting things Will is telling his jock buddies. Whatever he wants people to think, it's going to be all over school soon."

"So, what are you going to do?" Elizabeth asked.

Jessica looked into her sister's eyes. What she

really wanted was for Elizabeth to *tell* her what to do, but all she saw in her sister's face was pity. Being pitied was something Jessica wasn't used to. And she didn't like it.

Taking a deep breath, Jessica straightened herself up and pushed her hair behind her shoulders. "I'm going to go up to Will and tell him exactly what he can do with his stupid rumors. It's bad enough he lied to me. He's not going to get away with lying *about* me."

"Jess, I understand how you feel," Elizabeth said. "But if anyone sees you with him, it'll just give them more to talk about. And you know you'd lose it. It's a headline waiting to happen. 'Will's jilted lover throws a fit.' I think you should avoid him as much as possible."

Jessica's mounting frustration was making her want to jump out of her skin. "Then what am I supposed to do? Let them trash me as much as they want?"

"Maybe I should go talk to him," Elizabeth suggested.

"Right," Jessica scoffed. "That'd look good— sending in my sister to fight my battles. Why don't we just call Mom?"

"Just try to stay calm." Elizabeth looked down at Jessica's jittering leg, and Jessica forced it to stay still. "You know how you are, Jess. You always get caught up in these little social dramas like they were the end of the world. Eventually people just forget about it and life goes on. They'll start talking about something else unless you give them a reason to keep focusing on you."

"Whatever," Jessica said. She didn't understand how Elizabeth could always be so calm and logical about everything. Jessica had been betrayed—blindsided—and left with no viable options. Elizabeth wanted her to accept it.

"It might not seem like it right now," Elizabeth said, "but this will blow over soon. Sooner, if you just chill out." Elizabeth bit her bottom lip, then smiled. "Remember last year when everyone was talking about you falling down the stairs at the Bridgewater game and you skipped Lila's party because of it?"

Jessica managed a small smile. "And then Lila danced right into the table and fell into the punch bowl."

"No one ever mentioned your insignificant little trip again," Elizabeth reminded her.

"This is just slightly more serious than tripping down the stairs," Jessica pointed out.

"I know. But tomorrow some star soccer player will get caught drinking on campus or something and that'll be that."

Jessica shrugged, feeling helpless. Ignoring the problem went against her self-preservation instinct. But she knew that objectively, Elizabeth was making sense.

"Okay," she said finally, stretching out her arms to hug Elizabeth. She couldn't help wishing that she could look forward to going home and crying on her sister's shoulder. "I'll try not to make it a bigger deal than it is. I just have to remember who my friends are."

And who they aren't.

Elizabeth Wakefield

When you go crazy, do you <u>know</u> you're going crazy? Do you retain some objective part of yourself that watches it happen? Or does the fact that you're still thinking coherently enough to wonder if you're going crazy mean you're still sane?

Who knows if all those nineteenth-century writers who ended up stark raving mad ever stopped to think, "Hmmm, this poem is pretty out there. Maybe I better take it easy on the opium for a while." Or if Van Gogh said to himself, "Gee, I wonder if chicks <u>really</u> dig getting bloody, severed ears delivered to them in a box. Perhaps I should just stick to flowers and candy . . . nah. Too unoriginal."

What brought this on? Well, in the

past couple of days I've pretty much convinced myself that I'm certifiable. . . . Otherwise, how could I possibly explain my random infatuation with someone I can't stand?

Maybe I haven't been possessed with the urge to chop off any bodily appendages and give them to Conner. But I turn into a complete blithering idiot around him.

But then, maybe I'm not insane. I did promise myself I'd make some changes in my life this year. And if I've changed enough to fall for somebody like Conner, maybe it just means there's more to me than bland, predictable Elizabeth Wakefield.

Then again, maybe I've just taken the first step on a road that ends with my ear in a box.

CHAPTER 3
A Breath of Fresh Air

"So, what do you think?" Elizabeth asked Jessica as she roamed around Elizabeth's new bedroom on Monday afternoon.

"Is he always playing the guitar?" Jessica asked.

"I've only been here for a day," Elizabeth said with a laugh as she listened to Conner pluck away in the next room.

"Where's his mom?" Jessica asked, picking up an empty vase on the dresser and studying it. "And Megan."

"Mrs. Sandborn left a note that she would be at the country club, and Megan has soccer practice," Elizabeth answered. It was weird keeping tabs on someone else's family.

Jessica looked out the back window. "Do you like it here?" she asked, sounding a bit vulnerable.

"The room is great," Elizabeth said. "It's just weird. New people. New rules." *Like always knock before entering a room.*

"You know, you could still come over for dinner or something," Jessica said softly. "I know Mom and

Dad would love it, and I kind of miss having you around. I miss the way things used to be."

Elizabeth sighed. Living away from her sister was so strange. All their lives their rooms had been separated by nothing more than a bathroom—like she and Conner were now.

"Well, I miss you guys too," she said. "But I have a feeling that if I set foot in that house again, Lila will get one of the servants to poison me or something."

The phone rang, and Elizabeth jumped. The princess phone in her room was turned up to fire-alarm volume. Conner's music stopped.

"I should probably go," Jessica said. "I have to work tonight, and I want to shower and change before I go."

"Okay, so I'll see you—"

Conner's door slammed, and Elizabeth stopped midsentence. Jessica shot her a concerned look as they heard Conner barrel down the hallway and past Elizabeth's closed door, cursing all the way.

"Not a happy phone call, I guess," Jessica said after the front door closed.

"I guess not."

Elizabeth walked Jessica downstairs and hugged her good-bye at the door. "Call me later," she said.

"I will," Jessica said quietly.

Just as Jessica drove out of sight, another car pulled into the driveway. Elizabeth stood in the open doorway as two guys and a girl walked up the front path. She recognized one of the guys, a freckled redhead, from her writing class. He'd written a really funny commentary on body piercing. She drew a blank on strangers two and three.

The girl seemed surprised. "Hi . . . Jessica? What are you doing here?"

"Oh, I'm not Jessica," Elizabeth said quickly. She took in the fifties-style short-sleeved white dress with red cherry print and the clunky black Dr. Martens boots. The girl's dark hair was pulled back into a ponytail that tumbled in a mass of curls down her back. "We're twins. I'm Elizabeth."

"Right! The twins. I'm Tia Ramirez. I know your sister from cheerleading," the girl said. Elizabeth blinked. Tia was compact and athletic but didn't fit Elizabeth's image of the cheerleader type at all. "This is my boyfriend, Angel Desmond. He graduated last spring."

"What's up?" Angel said. He was a tall African American guy with close-trimmed hair, whose hand rested familiarly on Tia's hip. His easy grin was infectious.

"Nice to meet you," Elizabeth answered.

"And this is Andy Marsden," Tia said.

"You're the one in Quigley's class, right?" Freckles said. Elizabeth nodded. In his crew-neck navy shirt and jeans, he looked like a J. Crew guy. He stuffed his hands in his pockets. "So, Elizabeth, can Conner come out to play?"

"You just missed him." Elizabeth glanced over her shoulder toward the staircase as if Conner might suddenly reappear. "But you're welcome to wait here if you want."

"Thanks," Tia said. Elizabeth held open the door, and they filed into the Sandborns' front room.

Angel took a seat on the couch, and Tia sat down next to him. She cocked her head and looked at Elizabeth. "Conner mentioned you were staying here, but I didn't realize you were Jessica's sister. You moved in yesterday, right?"

"Yeah, Megan offered me the spare room last week," Elizabeth explained. "My house got wrecked in the quake."

"Oh, that sucks," Tia lamented. "We were lucky. The only thing that got smashed was my mother's collection of Hummel figurines, which was more of a blessing than a curse. Those things were hideous."

"Baby, you realize she's replacing them," Angel said gravely. "She made me look at catalogs with her for like an hour."

"When did this happen?" Tia shrieked, grabbing a magazine from the glass table and swatting him with it. "I swear you spend more time with my mother than with me." Angel grinned and snatched the magazine out of her hand. Tia swiped for it, and he gave her a quick kiss on the lips.

"Hanging out with you is like watching an episode of *The Love Boat*," Andy said dryly.

"Shut up, Marsden." Tia rolled her eyes, then turned to Elizabeth. "Ignore him. He's from a primitive culture that communicates exclusively in quote-unquote wacky one-liners."

Andy shot Elizabeth an amused look. "Aren't you glad you let us in? By the way, we're not ax murderers or anything. I mean, we'd tell you if we were."

Tia let out an exasperated sigh. "Cut it out, Andy. She thinks you're a freak."

"It's okay," Elizabeth said. "Some of my best friends are freaks." She exchanged a grin with Andy.

"Hey, what time is it?" Tia looked at her watch. "We told Conner five. Do you wanna just go and leave him a note?"

"Sounds like a plan." Angel nodded.

"Do you want to come?" Tia asked Elizabeth as Angel jotted the note. "We're just going to House of Java for a cup of coffee or whatever. But you're totally welcome to join us."

Elizabeth hesitated. She should really try to get some homework done. Her creative-writing notebook was calling her name . . . but Conner's friends seemed really cool. Andy didn't appear to be worried about *his* assignment.

"Sure!" she said finally. "I'd love to come."

"God, the service here is *terrible*," Elizabeth said loudly as a lanky waiter with short, black hair approached their table. "We've been waiting forever!"

37

Tia, Angel, and Andy stared at her, obviously embarrassed. Elizabeth grinned.

"Very funny, Liz," the waiter said. "If you want to show everybody what truly superior House of Java service looks like, you're welcome to take my shift for me, and I'll sit here and hang out with your friends."

"Okay, okay, I take it back," Elizabeth replied. "I work here part-time," she explained to the shocked group. "Jeremy, this is Tia, Angel, and Andy."

"We've never seen this girl before," Andy declared, offering Jeremy his hand. "She just sat down here with us and we were afraid to ask her to leave. She looks dangerously unstable."

Jeremy grinned as he shook Andy's hand, his dark brown eyes twinkling. "You wanna talk dangerously unstable, you should see her wrestling with the cappuccino machine. So, what can I get you guys?"

"I'll have an iced Mochaccino," Tia said promptly. "And Angel wants a French roast, milk, no sugar, and a cheese Danish."

"We spend way too much time together," Angel said solemnly, crooking an affectionate arm around Tia's neck.

"Not possible," Tia said. "You are leaving soon, remember?" She was smiling, but her tone had taken a turn toward the serious.

Andy ordered a decaf, and Jeremy scribbled on

his pad. "And for my esteemed colleague?" he asked, looking at Elizabeth.

Elizabeth laughed. "A latte. Thanks." Jeremy nodded and headed back toward the counter.

"Hey, sorry we dragged you to work," Angel said. "This is probably the last place you want to hang out."

"Oh, no, I don't mind," Elizabeth said sincerely. She glanced around the dimly lit coffeehouse, from the couches and overstuffed chairs scattered throughout the room to the Christmas lights and flyers lining the walls. "This is actually a pretty cool place when you don't have to deal with subduing a lot of pathologically caffeinated customers."

She was also aware that if Conner found the note they'd left, he might show up later. Elizabeth wiped the thought from her mind the moment it appeared. She was here making new friends, not stalking some guy.

"Yeah, I've always liked the élan of this place," Angel said reflectively, gazing in the direction of a large oil painting of a woman drinking coffee.

"Élan?" Tia repeated. "What kind of SAT word is that, Mr. Stanford? We already know you're intellectually superior. Do you have to rub it in?"

"Oh, give me a break." Angel pulled on one of Tia's many curls. "I'm starting at Stanford in January," he explained to Elizabeth. So that was why he was leaving. "She likes to make sure I don't get a big head about it."

39

"Are you kidding? Let the ego swell," Elizabeth said. "I'd be pretty psyched if I got into Stanford."

"I just wish they had some Ivy in southern California," Tia said. "So my man didn't have to chase it all the way up the coast."

Andy and Angel laughed, but Tia started toying with some sugar packets, obviously not all that amused.

Jeremy returned with their order. "And you better be a big tipper since I know you've got a glamorous, cushy job," he told Elizabeth with a wink.

Tia snapped out of her daze when Jeremy placed her coffee in front of her. "He's really cute," she whispered, leaning across the table toward Elizabeth as Jeremy walked away.

"Hey!" Angel said indignantly.

"I mean for Elizabeth, baby," Tia said. "Get real."

"They've been together since freshman year," Andy explained. "I don't think either of them even remembers that other members of the opposite sex exist."

"Well, can you blame me?" Tia asked. "Most members of the male species seem to have difficulty walking erect without dragging their knuckles on the ground. Am I right?"

"Studies have shown that, yes," Elizabeth commented.

Tia laughed, fully bubbly again. "Hey! You know what we should do? Elizabeth, have you ever been to the Riot?"

Elizabeth shook her head. She'd heard of the dance club where the El Carro kids hung out, but always assumed it wasn't her thing.

"It's an all-ages club," Angel explained. "Kind of like a rave scene."

"It's awesome," Tia said emphatically. "We have to take you. This week sometime, definitely. I don't know about you guys, but I feel like I haven't done anywhere near enough frolicking since senior year started."

"You can never do too much frolicking," Andy agreed.

"Are you in, Elizabeth?" Tia prodded.

"Sounds good," Elizabeth said, hoping she didn't have a big dopey smile on her face. It was flattering that they were including her so readily in their plans. Maybe the dweeby, boring Elizabeth Wakefield mold was already starting to crumble.

"I do not need a ride home," Mrs. Sandborn shouted, slapping Conner's hand away. "What I need is another drink." She glared at the country-club attendant behind the bar, who was trying his best to ignore her.

"Mom, you don't need another drink. It's time to go." Conner felt nauseous, both from the alcohol on his mother's breath and from his sinking sense of déjà vu. How many times had he gone through this exact same painfully embarrassing exchange with her?

"I'll give you a hand." Another club attendant who had been lingering nearby took one of Mrs. Sandborn's arms.

"Get off me," she said, yanking herself away. "I can walk fine." He backed off.

Conner grabbed her arm as she lost her footing getting down from the stool. She leaned against him. Conner tried not to stumble as they awkwardly made their way out of the clubhouse and through the parking lot to his car.

A thin, middle-aged man in a charcoal suit was standing by the Mustang, his arms folded peevishly across his chest. Conner recognized him as John Pierson, the club's social director, who had called earlier. He and Conner had an ongoing relationship.

"Mr. McDermott, I'll be blunt," Pierson said as Conner deposited his mother in the car. "Valley Stream has a reputation to uphold. As I'm sure you're aware, your mother's behavior has threatened that reputation on countless occasions. This is the third time this month we've had to call you out here."

"Fourth," Conner corrected.

Pierson's face barely veiled his contempt. "Regardless, we can no longer afford to look the other way while your mother disgraces herself and us. Since she doesn't appear to be in any condition to communicate right now, I would appreciate it if you would inform her that one more incident like this will be grounds for termination of her membership."

"I'll pass that along," Conner said evenly. He slid into the driver's seat and slammed the door.

The whole ride home Conner couldn't speak a word to his mother or even look at her. He hated himself for always being around to clean up her messes—always keeping her secrets and suffering her humiliations because she was too wasted to deal.

Sometimes he was tempted to quit trying. It would be so easy to just drop out of school and walk away from his life. It wasn't like his mother would notice. All he was to her was a designated driver. But he couldn't do that to Megan, couldn't leave her with the horrible burden of being their mother's baby-sitter.

When they pulled up to the house, Conner opened his mother's door and dragged her to her feet. He slung her limp arm around his shoulders and felt her body shift, leaning on him like a deadweight. She was completely passed out. Conner staggered unsteadily forward, zigzagging with his mother to the front door.

God, please let Elizabeth stay in her room, he prayed silently as he fumbled with his keys. He could only imagine what she would think of his mother's disgusting spectacle.

But he found the house darkened and still. Relieved, Conner flipped on the light and dragged his mother into the living room. "Come on, Mom, let's get you upstairs," he said wearily.

As they passed the coffee table, Conner caught sight of a sheet of notebook paper.

C.—

Meet Tia, Andy, Elizabeth, and me at House of Java.

Angel

Conner hefted his mother's weight onto the first stair. So Elizabeth was hanging out with Andy and Tia now. Well, whatever. At least she was out of the house. And out of his face.

He had just heaved his mother to the top of the stairs and was pausing for a moment to catch his breath when he heard the front door open again.

"Anybody home?" Elizabeth's chipper little voice called out. Conner cursed under his breath.

Suddenly alert, Mrs. Sandborn lifted her head and let out a garbled cry. "Megan, zzzat you?"

"Shut *up!*" Conner hissed between clenched teeth, pushing his mother down the hall toward her bedroom. "Just be quiet, Mom. It's time for you to lie down."

"But I—" Conner heard footsteps on the staircase. His heart began to pound. Frantically he hustled his mother to her bedroom, opened the door, and practically pushed her inside.

"Just go to sleep, okay?" he whispered before closing the door. A muffled groan replied.

"Hi!" a voice behind him sang out. Conner turned as Elizabeth poked her head into the upstairs hallway. Her eyes were dancing.

"I just had a great time with . . ." She trailed off, evidently noticing that Conner was standing guard in front of his mother's room, his back rigid against the door.

Elizabeth's brows knitted in concern. "Is everything all right?"

Conner felt fury rising in his chest.

"Everything's fine," he said curtly. "Everything *would* be fine if you'd just mind your own damn business."

Conner turned on his heel and stomped down the hall to his room, but not before catching a glimpse of the crestfallen look on Elizabeth's face.

He closed his door behind him and sank to the floor, burying his face in his hands.

He hated his mother. He hated her for being a drunk. He hated her for putting him in this position time and time again. He hated himself for letting her.

He hated Elizabeth too. For waltzing into his life all bright eyed and innocent. And for threatening to blow open the secret he'd sacrificed so much to keep covered.

"I don't see what the big deal is," Cherie Reese declared, munching on a carrot stick. "She's not even that good."

45

"That good at what?" Gina Cho asked.

Melissa knitted her brow. "Cherie, you're eating like Bugs Bunny," she said. Cherie's cheeks flushed, and she put the rest of her carrot down on her plate.

"At cheerleading, duh," she answered Gina.

"She *is* that good," Melissa said, not grudgingly, but matter-of-factly. It was never productive to underestimate the competition.

Lila shifted in her seat and took a sip of her soda. "I like this place," she said, looking around at Rafferty's seventies-throwback decor. Melissa eyed Lila, who was obviously trying to change the subject. She'd thought Lila had decided to cut ties with Jessica, but after the way she'd chased Jessica out of class . . . Lila was obviously even more loyal than Melissa had originally thought. Still, she was here now. Melissa was glad she'd thought to invite Lila and Amy to her friends' traditional Monday-night dinner out.

"Yeah. We've been coming here for three years," Melissa said. "All the SVH hangouts are lame."

Amy Sutton smiled her accommodating smile. She'd been much easier to win over than Lila. "We should come here more often," Amy said.

Melissa nodded as she sipped her diet soda.

"But she's not in your league, Liss," Gina insisted, mercifully returning to the conversation at hand. "You'll definitely make captain over her. Don't even worry about it."

"We'll find out soon enough, I guess." Melissa

46

rapped absently on the wooden tabletop. She wanted to warn Gina not to jinx it, but that would have sounded ridiculous.

"And she's not even that pretty either," Cherie asserted, straightening up. She reached back to pull her mass of auburn curls into a ponytail. "I mean, she's that cheesy kind of pretty, like a model at a car show or something."

"Pretty enough for Will," Melissa said softly. Peripherally she saw Cherie and Gina exchange a worried look.

"Guys don't actually *like* those kind of girls, Liss—they can just tell they're not a challenge," Cherie said decisively. "I mean, do you really think Will would pick trash like that over you?"

"Come on, just look at what she had on today," Gina said. She was studying her hands as she spoke, meticulously wiping off each finger. "Um . . . 1985 called—they want your outfit back."

Lila pushed her straight brown hair behind her ears. "That was my outfit," she said.

Gina didn't even flinch. She scrubbed at her thumb. "Well, obviously it would look classy on you."

Lila smirked and shook her head. "Obviously," she echoed.

"I can't believe she never came back to class today," Cherie said. "What a loser."

"Seriously," Amy said, even though she hadn't been there.

47

"Who wrote that on the board anyway?" Lila asked nonchalantly. She started studying her own nails. Melissa looked at Cherie and knew her best friend was sharing her thoughts. How much would Lila tell Jessica? And did they really care if Jessica knew they'd done it? Out of the corner of her eye she saw Lila watching them. She knew the girl was forming her own opinions about what Melissa and Cherie were thinking—and probably coming to the correct conclusion.

"The guys did," Cherie said finally, leaning back in her chair. "They *are* the ones with first-hand knowledge of Jessica's . . . habits."

Melissa hid a grin behind her napkin. Sometimes she really wondered if she and Cherie had a psychic connection. She stifled a laugh at the idea.

"What did she say when you caught up with her?" Gina asked, glancing at Melissa before she looked at Lila. Okay, so maybe Gina was in on the ESP too.

Lila pushed her plate of salad away. She smiled weakly at Melissa. "She was pretty much babbling incoherently."

Melissa shot Cherie another glance and smiled. She popped a french fry into her mouth and smiled. There was still hope for Lila.

Elizabeth Wakefield

Reasons to Stay Away from Conner

1. He's totally obnoxious and has no idea how to treat people—especially guests in his own house.
2. You are a guest in his house, and if anything ever did happen, his mom would probably boot you for taking advantage of her hospitality.
3. "Hi, Mom! This is my boyfriend . . . who I'm living with."
4. Maria likes him.
5. After 4, I don't really need a 5, do I?

Conner McDermott

Creative Writing
<u>Character</u> <u>Study</u>

Evan Mulroney had figured out when he was still just a kid that the worst advice people gave was, "Just be yourself." It didn't take long before he understood that being yourself was the most pitiful move you could make.

Evan wasn't a fake. He just made a point of keeping what he <u>was</u> to himself.

Seeing what made people tick was boring at best, depressing at worst. Nothing could be more pathetic than the losers on talk shows who bawled about their traumatic childhoods, their negligent parents, their tragic lives.

Evan saw people he knew pulling that emotional crap all the time, and he hated how weak it made them look. He'd be damned if he was going to open himself up that way. Revealing yourself meant revealing weakness.

He had found that if he kept to himself, if he gave nothing, people stayed away. People were usually so insecure, they just assumed if he was aloof, he must somehow be better than them. They projected their own idealized images onto him. And all Evan had to do to live up to those images was not be himself.

Evan undoubtedly felt alone sometimes. But it was better to be alone by choice than to end up being left alone.

CHAPTER
Raw Nerves
4

"I really like Elizabeth," Tia announced as she slid into the passenger seat of Angel's battered Toyota after dropping Elizabeth off on Monday night. "She seems so . . . not fake."

"Could you open that door again and slam it a little more loudly?" Andy complained from the backseat. Tia turned around and stuck out her tongue at him.

"Not fake as opposed to what?" Angel asked, starting the engine.

"As opposed to—I don't know. Conner was telling me how he ran into these blond twins who were total California stereotypes, 'like, you know, omigod!' And Elizabeth isn't that way at all."

"No, definitely not," Angel agreed. "She seems real down-to-earth. I'm glad there are some cool people at your new school."

He looked at Tia, and they smiled their harmonious smile at each other.

"Angel, you have a lot of crap in your backseat," Andy said. Tia looked back and saw him pushing a sweatshirt and a pile of papers to the side. "What is all this stuff?"

Angel looked in the rearview mirror. "Just a bunch of paperwork from Stanford. My housing assignment and stuff like that."

Andy held up a blue card. "Is this where you're living? Kimball Hall?"

"Yeah, I guess," Angel said. "I'm supposed to sign a bunch of forms and put down a deposit."

Forms. Signatures. Deposits. Tia felt her good mood wane. She reached into the backseat. "Let me see." Andy handed her the card.

Gingerly Tia fingered the blue three-by-five card imprinted in elegant letters with Stanford University Housing Assignment Services. She studied the affixed sticky label that read *Angel Desmond, 113 Kimball Hall*. The computer-generated print seemed so impersonal and final. He was in their system now. This was really happening.

Andy affected a noxious surfer-dude inflection. "So is that, like, the party dorm, man?"

"Nobody at Stanford parties," Angel said. "They all just study or play tennis."

"Liar. You're going to leave me for some incredibly hot college woman you meet at a keg party," Tia said in a plaintive voice that came out sounding a little less joking than she'd intended.

"Aw, don't even say that, Tee," Angel said, reaching out to squeeze her shoulder.

"Angel's so whipped, he could take a class with a supermodel and not concentrate on anything except his notes," Andy said with good-natured disgust.

"He's got a point," Angel said.

"I just can't believe you're going, that's all," Tia said with a sigh.

Angel slipped his hand beneath her thick blanket of hair and tickled her neck lightly with his fingertips. "What did you think I filled out all those applications for?"

"I know, I know." She bit her lip. "Forget I said anything." There was a pause in the conversation, and Tia saw Angel meet Andy's eyes in the mirror. Great. They probably thought she was about to get all melodramatic on them.

"So, Angel, are you stuck with a roommate?" Andy asked.

"I think so," Angel answered. Tia tuned out as they began to discuss the many possible ways a randomly assigned roommate could manifest psychosis.

She wished she hadn't let on to Angel how completely unprepared she was for him leaving for Stanford. Over the summer it had been so easy to make herself forget he was going away. With the earthquake and then the news about having to move to SVH, she'd had plenty of other worries to occupy her mind. Besides, the whole point of him deferring a semester was so he could earn enough working at his dad's auto body shop to afford weekend and vacation visits. As an abstract prospect, that had seemed manageable.

But now, holding the benign blue housing card, it hit her that Angel wasn't just starting a new school like she was. He was moving to a new city. He would essentially have a whole new home. Weekends and vacations weren't the same as seeing him day in and day out.

"But most dorms there are coed, aren't they?" Andy asked.

Lovely. Giggling girls probably scampered down the corridors of Kimball Hall clad in towels. No doubt they'd be knocking on Angel's doors at all hours.

Tia looked sideways at Angel, fear beginning to nip at her spine at the thought of the left-behind-girlfriend existence. How was she going to face the prospect of indefinite months of loneliness while Angel partied until dawn in room 113, Kimball Hall?

"Perfect," Elizabeth moaned as she looked at her watch.

So far, this Tuesday morning was one for the record books. She'd slept through her alarm for the first time in . . . basically her entire life. There had been no hot water for her shower, she'd poured a cup of sour milk onto her Frosted Flakes, and now she'd missed the bus. Her only possible transport was the guy she'd been avoiding all morning. The last thing she wanted was to get her head bitten off—again.

Elizabeth heard the Mustang engine revving in the driveway and decided to bite the bullet. She opened the door and strode out to the driveway as confidently as possible. Luckily the passenger-side window was rolled down. Elizabeth leaned over and looked at Conner.

"Hi," she said. "I guess Megan took the bus without me."

"She left a while ago. She walks to school with some of the other girls from the soccer team sometimes," Conner said. He surveyed her in silence for a moment. "Need a ride?" he asked finally.

"Thanks," Elizabeth said. She pulled at the door handle once, twice. It didn't open.

Conner leaned over with a smirk and easily popped the door. "Trick handle," he said.

"Oh." Elizabeth climbed in and slammed the door. Definitely record-book material. "This has been the worst morning—"

She turned toward Conner at the exact moment he twisted his torso around to glance behind them. Her nose was practically touching the center of his chest. Elizabeth pushed herself back into her seat, but not before smelling the light but distinctly male scent of his aftershave. He briefly rested his hand on Elizabeth's headrest, and her scalp tingled. She couldn't remember ever being this close to him before.

Get a grip! She forced her eyes to stare straight

ahead. If she didn't move or speak, there was a slim possibility she could avoid making an idiot of herself before they got to school.

"Worst morning?" Conner asked as he shifted gears.

"Never mind," Elizabeth said.

He leaned over to turn the radio dial, and as he withdrew his arm, it brushed against Elizabeth's knee. Suddenly she had a vivid flash of the dream she'd been having when her alarm went off. She and Conner . . . There had definitely been lips and hands and fingertips involved. That was why she hadn't wanted to wake up.

Elizabeth glanced down at Conner's fingers, wrapped around the gearshift. She almost reached out and placed her hand over his just to see how it felt. She looked out the window instead.

When Elizabeth was a little girl and her parents took her to museums, she would always instinctively clasp her hands behind her back, fighting the forbidden urge to lay her palms flat on the cool marble of the statues, to run her fingers along the lush, valleyed surfaces of paintings. There was something maddening about being in the presence of such beautiful things, yet not being allowed to experience them with all her senses.

Now, sitting so close to Conner, she had a similar impulse. It was senseless. Totally, completely, and in all other ways wrong. Conner had been so blatantly mean to her the night before. In fact, he'd been nothing but rude and sarcastic to her since the day they'd met. And he was obviously totally guarded—someone who would be impossible to get close to even if she tried. Elizabeth wanted honesty and openness in her relationships. All of them.

But she'd never been so physically drawn to anyone before, not like this. It just didn't make any sense.

Conner eased the car into the SVH parking lot and pulled into a space. He cut the engine and turned to Elizabeth. She flashed on an image of him leaning in to kiss her—slowly—seductively.

"Thanks for the ride," she said automatically.

"You already thanked me." His voice had softened a little.

"Oh. Right. Well. I guess I'll see you around," Elizabeth mumbled, not looking in Conner's direction. She reached again for the door handle and pulled at it two seconds before she remembered the thing was broken. *What an idiot.*

"Up and left," Conner said.

Elizabeth froze. "What?" she blurted, a bit too loudly.

"The handle. You have to pull it up and left," Conner said, half smiling. "Trick handle, remember?"

"Right. Thanks," Elizabeth said. She popped the door and practically tumbled out of the car.

*   *   *

59

"Thanks for the ride, Li," Jessica said, holding her hair back against the wind. There was nothing more therapeutic than zipping through town in a new Porsche convertible on a beautiful California morning. Jessica almost felt like yesterday hadn't happened.

"No problem," Lila said, downshifting as she took a corner. "I wanted to talk to you anyway."

Jessica reached into her backpack on the floor and started searching for a headband. "What's up?" she asked.

"I just wanted to make sure you were okay," Lila said, glancing away from the road to look at Jessica. "I was worried when you never came back to class yesterday. And then you disappeared right after school."

Jessica pushed the headband into her bangs. "I know. I went to Elizabeth's." She turned to Lila. "How does this look?"

"Take it off when we get there," Lila said.

Jessica flipped down the visor and checked her hair in the vanity mirror. It was pretty nerdy. In fact, her whole outfit could have been lifted from Elizabeth's wardrobe. Plain, not so formfitting blue jeans and a red-and-blue-striped T-shirt. She was barely even wearing any makeup. At least her thick-soled, blue-suede sneakers were semicool. Although being mistaken for Elizabeth would probably be a relief at this point.

"Anyway, I just don't want you to get all wiggy before tryouts," Lila said.

Jessica squinted at her friend. "Why would I get wiggy?"

Lila pulled into the SVH parking lot and narrowly avoided running over a couple of football players. "Because of Melissa," Lila said. "You know that girl wants the captainship. And she's really good."

Jessica's heart flopped. "Yeah, but—"

"And she's totally popular," Lila said, adjusting the sleeves of her leopard-print jacket. "I mean, people really like her."

"You don't think she's going to get it, do you?" Jessica asked. She was starting to regret breakfast. Her stomach was screaming for Pepto-Bismol. "You don't think Laufeld would really do that?"

Lila cut the engine and turned to Jessica. "No! No! Definitely not." She pushed her designer sunglasses back on her head.

"Because you sound like you're on her side all of a sudden," Jessica said.

Lila touched Jessica's shoulder. "Okay, you're totally misunderstanding me. All I said was, I was worried that *you* might be worried." She hit the button that automatically raised the roof. "And you shouldn't be because Melissa has nothing on you."

"Okay . . ." This conversation was confusing Jessica.

"Seriously, Jessica, I mean it," Lila said as the

roof snapped into place, blocking out the sun. "Everything's going to be fine." Lila climbed out of the car and slammed the door, shaking the tiny automobile.

Jessica numbly stared through the windshield as students filed through the front door of the school. Suddenly she really didn't want to go in there.

Elizabeth Wakefield

Creative Writing
<u>Character</u> <u>Study</u>

Lea Jessup had always had one, good, true friend. Mara Sanders. And she was grateful for that blessing. She never needed to be surrounded by a huge group of people because she knew they'd do her no good. She knew that to be part of a crowd meant just that—one of many—and no one really cared about who the others in the crowd were. Not for real.

But now Lea's life was starting to change. There were new people. People who didn't seem like a stereotypical group. People who seemed to want to know Lea. And suddenly her one friendship with Mara seemed old, tired, tarnished. Boring.

This feeling made Lea do things she wouldn't normally do. She still loved her one true friend, and she still wanted what was best for her. But she was also starting to wonder what was best for herself. It was hard for Lea, who had always seen the distinction between right and wrong very clearly. Now the distinction was fading, and Lea didn't like the feeling.

She didn't like it at all.

CHAPTER 5

Drawing Lines

"Did you finish your article for the meeting?" Elizabeth asked Megan as they walked toward the *Oracle* office on Tuesday afternoon.

"Finally." Megan blushed. "I would've shown it to you last night, but I finished in study hall about five seconds ago."

"That's okay," Elizabeth said. "I haven't even written my letter-from-the-editor thing yet."

"Hey, foxy mamas!" a girl's voice called.

Tensing, Elizabeth whirled around, trying to formulate a scathing comeback. But the words died in her throat when she saw Tia and Andy walking down the corridor toward her and Megan.

Elizabeth exhaled in a laugh, the mental image of Jessica's tormentors fading. "God, you guys."

"Friends! Friends!" Andy said, throwing one arm around Elizabeth's shoulders and the other around Megan's. "You look like two girls who could use a little R and R at the mall."

"What a coincidence!" Tia exclaimed breathlessly.

"That's exactly where we were headed. Isn't that amazing?"

"I think it's amazing," Andy repeated.

"Unreal," Elizabeth agreed as Megan laughed.

"So, let's go," Tia said, quickly tugging on Elizabeth's sleeve. "I need something for the Riot. I'm so sick of everything I own."

"Yeah, come with us," Andy urged, grabbing Megan's books out of her hands. "Don't make me bear the entire burden of being Tia's fashion adviser. She always buys stuff she doesn't like and ends up blaming me."

"We can't," Megan said. "We have an *Oracle* meeting."

Mr. Collins, the *Oracle*'s adviser, popped his head out of the office. "Are you girls coming?" Megan took her books back from Andy and walked through the door as Mr. Collins held it open.

Elizabeth glanced at her watch. "Hey! I've got ten minutes," she told Mr. Collins.

He smiled. "Always getting me on technicalities." He walked back into the office, closing the door behind him.

"Sorry," Elizabeth told Tia and Andy.

Tia overacted shocked. "You'd rather discuss headlines than hemlines?" Elizabeth laughed. Tia sounded just like Jessica.

"Well, when you put it that way . . ." Maybe she could come up with an excuse for Mr. Collins. "Why not?" Elizabeth said, slinging her backpack over her shoulder. She glanced down at her cotton T-shirt and jeans. "I could use a minor overhaul myself."

"Makeovers are good for the soul," Tia announced.

Elizabeth stuck her head into the *Oracle* office. "Mr. Collins, I just remembered I have to work today," she said. Her heart pounded, anticipating his disapproval.

He looked up from his desk. "I thought you had off on Tuesdays so you could be here," he said.

"I know." Elizabeth swallowed with difficulty. "The manager messed up the schedule this week. It won't happen again."

"All right, then, I'll hold down the fort."

"Thanks, Mr. C." Elizabeth caught a glimpse of Megan's perplexed expression before the door closed. She turned to look at her friends, surprised at how easily she'd made her escape. "You guys are going to have to pay for the honor of my company," Elizabeth quipped.

"Oh, really?" Andy said as they started down the hallway. "How?"

"In the form of ice cream," Elizabeth answered.

"I knew I liked her," Tia said.

Elizabeth smiled and realized there was a little bit of bounce to her step.

"Hey, Liz! Where're you going?"

Elizabeth stopped in her tracks and turned to

find Maria walking toward her. "Hey!" Elizabeth said. As Maria approached, she flicked her eyes from Elizabeth to her friends and back again.

"Maria, this is Tia and Andy," Elizabeth said. "Guys, this is Maria Slater." *Maria will be playing the role of my conscience,* Elizabeth predicted silently.

"Hi," Maria said tentatively.

Elizabeth hesitated. Maria wasn't her usual boisterous self. "Uh, we're on our way to the mall," she explained.

Maria's mouth dropped open slightly. "But we have an *Oracle* meeting."

"I know," Elizabeth said. Why did Maria have to look so shocked? "I'm just gonna bail. We're not really doing anything important today." Elizabeth prayed Maria wouldn't point out how un-Liz-like she was acting in front of her new friends. She sort of felt like being un-Liz today.

But Maria just raised her eyebrows and said nothing.

"Wanna come with us?" Tia suggested, flashing Maria a brilliant, dimpled smile.

"Yeah, Maria! You should come!" Elizabeth added, trying to sound enthusiastic.

Maria shook her head. "Thanks, but I really need to be at this meeting. If I don't assign some reviews, the next issue isn't going to have an arts section."

Elizabeth found herself letting out her breath, although she hadn't been aware she was holding it.

She smiled at Maria. "Well, if you're going to go anyway, there's a list of features on my desk. If you wouldn't mind, you could just go ahead and assign stuff. I trust your judgment."

Maria stared at Elizabeth as if she just suggested Maria choose a journalist to report on the White House.

Elizabeth shifted her weight uncomfortably. "Listen, if it's a big deal, never mind. I just thought—"

"No, it's fine. I'll do it." Maria pressed the words together into a flat line. "I'd better run. Nice meeting you." She nodded stiffly at Tia and Andy. She turned, pushed through the door to the *Oracle* office, and let it slam behind her.

"You too!" Tia called after her.

"Rejected," Andy said, hanging his head. "What a buzz kill."

"Yeah. I wish she'd come," Elizabeth said half-heartedly. But as they made their way down the stairs, Elizabeth felt a strange sense of relief. She was actually glad that Maria hadn't joined them. She probably would have spent the whole afternoon obsessing about college applications or feeling guilty over missing the meeting. And Elizabeth didn't want to feel guilty. She just wanted to feel free and have a little fun—and somehow it was easier around Tia and Andy. There was something liberating about hanging out with people who didn't know her at all.

* * *

Elizabeth shuffled on bare feet into the kitchen and flicked on the overhead light. It was almost one in the morning. Earlier, at the mall, her logic had taken a leave of absence, allowing Elizabeth to down an espresso. As if she hadn't been wound up enough lately.

Elizabeth scanned the contents of the refrigerator, took out a carton of milk, and poured herself a glass. She bent to put the carton back on the shelf and paused to see if there were any leftovers she felt like snacking on.

"Nice nightgown."

Elizabeth whirled around, startled by Conner's voice. Her glass slipped from her hand and crashed to the floor, spattering milk and glass shards across the linoleum. But Elizabeth barely even registered the crash.

Conner was leaning against the counter across the room, his arms folded across his bare chest. He had on a pair of gray boxer shorts . . . and nothing else.

For a long moment Elizabeth couldn't move. She vaguely realized that she should pick up the broken glass, but her pounding heart was the only part of her capable of movement.

Conner's eyes traveled slowly downward. Suddenly Elizabeth was acutely aware of the short, white baby-doll nightie she was wearing. She grabbed instinctively at the hem of her nightgown and yanked it down with both hands.

70

Elizabeth had the strange sensation of being totally exposed—and not just because of how she was dressed. It was as if Conner was seeing some part of her that nobody else could see, a part she barely knew was there. Something in his expression—something she didn't understand but that she *sensed* in her gut, or maybe in her heart—told her that he understood things she could only guess. She felt as if the two of them were standing still in time, two points bound together by an invisible line.

No, you're standing half naked in a kitchen, surrounded by broken glass, Elizabeth's rational mind interjected.

Her mouth had gone bone-dry. "You scared me," she finally managed, hoarsely.

Conner raised his eyebrows. "I gathered," he said in a low voice that sent shivers down Elizabeth's spine.

"So I'd better clean this up," she said. She knelt, taking care to tuck her nightgown under her knees, and began gingerly picking up pieces of glass.

Conner squatted beside her and did the same. His head was bent close to hers. "Be careful," he said without looking at her, so softly it was almost a whisper.

Elizabeth reached for a jagged glass shard. Conner was so near, she could feel the warmth of his body. She fought to keep from staring at his muscular arms—the bare, tanned expanse of his

71

back. If she turned her face toward his just a few inches, she could press her lips against his. . . .

Should I? Elizabeth wondered dizzily, feeling as if she were drifting through a dream. It would be so easy—just a slight, almost imperceptible motion. *Could I?*

It was an insane idea. But at that moment she couldn't recall *why* exactly it was such an insane idea. Elizabeth was conscious of nothing but Conner's total dominance of her personal space.

Then Conner's hand brushed hers and he jerked it away, breaking through the hopeful haziness of Elizabeth's dream world. "I'll get the mop," he said flatly. Elizabeth slammed back to reality.

Slowly, shakily, she got to her feet. *What were you thinking?* her mind screamed as Conner's broad, lightly freckled back disappeared into the pantry. She'd actually been on the verge of making a huge fool of herself. It was one thing to be attracted to him—she was human, after all. But what had possessed her even to think about making a move on Conner?

Looking down at the pile of glass she was holding, Elizabeth realized that her hands were trembling. What was happening to her? Guys were supposed to be the ones who sometimes had trouble thinking with their brains.

"What part of the cow is the brisket from anyway?" Cherie leaned over her tray and wrinkled her nose at the plates of sliced gray meat covered in gray gravy. "Apparently Wednesday is 'scare the students into dieting' day."

Melissa narrowed her eyes, glared at the back of Cherie's head, and tapped her foot impatiently on the floor. The sound was lost in the lunchroom din of plates and voices. Cherie continued scrutinizing the cafeteria counter, oblivious to the fact that Melissa was in a hurry.

"Why don't you just get a sandwich?" Gina volunteered.

Cherie sighed and slid her tray past the brisket station. "I know we always used to bitch about our old caf, but you have to admit it was much better than this."

"Well, our old caf is a pile of bricks." The words came out a little more snappish than Melissa had intended. "Just pick something so we can go sit down."

Gina and Cherie exchanged a look. Cherie picked a plastic-wrapped tuna sandwich from a pile and dropped it onto her tray. "Did someone miss her nap today?"

"Sorry, I'm just starving." Melissa smiled soothingly at her friends as they continued down the line toward the registers. She had to watch herself, no matter how thickheaded Cherie could be sometimes or how sick Melissa was of hearing—and thinking—about how much they all missed El Carro. She needed her friends, depended on their support. She couldn't afford to cop an attitude with them right now.

Melissa chewed her lip nervously as the lunch lady rang up her purchases. She glanced over at her friends at the next register, studying Cherie's stubby, compulsively bitten nails with their ragged dots of chipped pink polish; Gina's straight-out-of-a-magazine haircut. Some things never changed—including Cherie and Gina's loyalty.

Her friends had been so supportive over the past few days. They'd stuck by her decision to stay with Will even though Melissa was pretty sure he'd lied to her about not fooling around with Jessica Wakefield. And they'd helped her figure out how to deal with the whole Jessica situation—how to make sure Jessica would no longer pose a threat. Loyalty was one thing, but voluntarily drawing lines, alienating people at a new school, was another.

"Ready?" Melissa asked as she picked up her tray.

Cherie pushed a stray red curl out of her face, and it popped right back to where it had been a second before. She laughed and rolled her eyes. "Let's go."

Melissa's nerves eased as she scanned the crowd and zeroed in on what she was looking for. Lila Fowler, Amy Sutton, and several other girls from tryouts were sitting at a table near the middle of the room. Thankfully, Jessica wasn't with them.

"Oh, look," Cherie said smoothly. "There's a bunch of girls from cheerleading. Let's go sit with them."

Melissa smiled as they cut across the lunchroom. Okay, Cherie wasn't all *that* thickheaded.

Flanked by Cherie and Gina, Melissa set down her tray. "Mind if we join you?"

She landed, still smiling, in the seat across from Lila and looked up in time to see Jessica Wakefield standing frozen a few yards away. The girl was clutching her tray and staring aghast at Melissa as if she had just stolen her best friend.

Maria Slater, Sweet Valley, CA

YALE UNIVERSITY EARLY DECISION APPLICATION

Essay 1: Why do you think you are a qualified Yale applicant? What do you have to offer our institution? What qualities would you bring to the student body? What are your strengths, and what are your areas for improvement? (200 words or less)

I feel that I am extremely qualified to be a Yale student because I am intelligent, ambitious, and a self-starter. I would offer a great deal of . . .

What qualifies me to be a Yale student is that I am a conscientious student with an inquisitive mind and . . .

I am eminently qualified to be a Yale student for a number of reasons. The most evident one is . . .

Okay, here it is in a nutshell. The reason I'm qualified to be a Yale student is obvious from the fact that I'm sitting here on a perfectly gorgeous evening, at the start of senior year, slaving over my applications when every single person I know is out having fun. If I'm not dedicated enough to get into Yale, then who is? I mean, it's seventy-five degrees and still light outside, and here I am holed up in my room, cultivating my carpal tunnel syndrome. If nothing else, I belong at an Ivy League school simply because the weather on the West Coast is wasted on me.

What do I have to offer? Well, I guess I'd have to say that I could set a new standard with my overwhelming dorkiness. Guys whose idea of a wild night is posting jokes to the Dilbert news group would be taking nerd pointers from me. I'd make a great addition to the student body since my incredibly boring personality wouldn't distract anyone else from their studies. Like, after talking to me for five minutes, my roommate would probably flee to the library in search of some stimulation. It's an empirically proven fact that during conversations with me, people can physically _feel_ their youth slipping away.

Don't think I'm exaggerating either even my best friend, Elizabeth, has decided she's too cool to hang out with me. And if you're more straightlaced than Elizabeth Wakefield, you've got a problem.

CHAPTER
Only Human

6

What do I do now? Jessica clutched her tray as if rigor mortis had set into her fingers. Melissa was folding her napkin primly across her lap, smiling her cold-eyed smile at Lila. Cherie was laughing, too loudly. Amy laughed in response.

"Get a grip, Wakefield," she muttered under her breath. She couldn't go sit with her friends now. The last thing she wanted was to get into it with Melissa.

Jessica felt suddenly, horribly conspicuous standing at the front of the cafeteria, alone. She was a senior, not some lame freshman. She wasn't supposed to be drifting forlornly around the lunchroom, looking for a friend.

Jessica spotted Annie Whitman and Jade Wu and took a step toward them, then saw that they were sitting with a bunch of ECH girls from cheerleading.

Scratch that. She stepped back awkwardly. Todd Wilkins and Aaron Dallas were seated at the noisy table of jocks in the middle of the room. But

Will Simmons and his buddies were all there too.

There wasn't a solid block of familiar faces anywhere in the cafeteria. Ken Matthews, her ex-boyfriend, was sitting by himself in a corner, but Jessica hadn't spoken to him since Olivia's funeral. He didn't look like he wanted to be disturbed anyway. Jessica could practically see the dark cloud over his head.

Just start walking, she told herself. She forced her feet into action. But as she maneuvered around the room, panic started to set in. Even Elizabeth was nowhere to be found.

Behind her Jessica heard a wolf whistle and a harsh explosion of male laughter. She cringed, but willed herself not to turn around. *I give up.* All she wanted was to run.

Just then Jessica spied Maria Slater at a table on the right side of the cafeteria. She sighed in relief. A destination. She and Maria weren't really friends, but where Maria was sitting, Elizabeth was likely to show up.

Jessica sat down in an empty seat near Maria, who was picking listlessly at a salad. "Hey, what's up?" she said breathlessly. "Have you seen Liz?"

Maria made a snorting noise. "Actually, I was going to ask you the same thing."

"Oh." Jessica picked up her tuna sandwich and took a bite. She felt unequal to the task of filling the air with small talk, and Maria didn't look like she was in a particularly chatty mood either.

Jessica listened, detached, to the laughter and animated voices all around her. She felt isolated, forced to become an observer to the world of which she used to be the star. She'd become an outsider in her own school. It wasn't fair.

A strange, hollow feeling welled up inside Jessica's chest, making it hard for her to swallow. It took a moment for Jessica to identify the alien emotion, but then the realization hit her with enough force to make her slouch down in her chair.

For the first time she could remember, Jessica was lonely.

Maria took a deep breath as she approached Elizabeth's locker. She was going to be really casual and mellow. It was no big deal. Just because they ate lunch together practically every day didn't mean that today Elizabeth was purposely avoiding her.

And it was probably just a coincidence that Elizabeth seemed to be too busy every time Maria invited her to hang out, even though she dropped everything to hang out with her *new* friends— and dumped her *Oracle* responsibilities on Maria, like she was Elizabeth's personal assistant or something. Yep. A big coincidence.

"Hey, Liz!" Maria chirped cheerfully. That had sounded okay, hadn't it? Of course it had. She was an actress. This was a cinch.

Elizabeth looked up. "Oh, hey, Maria," she said, stuffing a notebook into her backpack. "What's up?"

"Cute shirt." Maria gestured toward Elizabeth's trendier-than-thou pale blue baby tee. A row of little red stars ran across the chest. "Is it new?"

"Yeah, thanks." Elizabeth glanced down. "I got it at the mall with Tia and Andy yesterday. I wasn't sure if it was me, but Tia talked me into it."

Tia. Couldn't Elizabeth go two seconds without mentioning her?

"So, I looked for you at lunch today," Maria said, keeping the accusation out of her voice. "Where were you?"

"Oh! Right," Elizabeth said, closing her eyes. "I'm sorry. I ditched lunch and went to get pizza with Tia and Angel. I should've found you and seen if you wanted to come."

Angel? Who the heck was *that*?

"That's okay. I was just asking," Maria said quickly, hating the tone of her own voice. She sounded like a jealous girlfriend. "So, do you want to do something tonight?" Maria asked.

"I can't tonight." Elizabeth shrugged apologetically. "Jeremy, this guy I work with at House of Java, got Radiohead tickets and asked me to cover his shift. He promised to take my next Sunday shift, and that's our most insane day, so I couldn't say no."

Okay, Maria would *not* take it personally. She would try one more time, and if Elizabeth had another lame excuse, *then* she would take it personally. "How about tomorrow?" she asked, her voice a little higher than natural.

"Oh, well, tomorrow I'm going to the Riot with Tia and Andy." Elizabeth hesitated for a split second before adding, "Do you want to come?"

Maria let out her breath and smiled gratefully at Elizabeth. "Sure, I'd love to."

"Cool." Elizabeth smiled back. "It should be fun. I really want you to get a chance to hang out with them."

"Yeah, great." Maria was relieved. "We'd better get to class. I'll give you a call to make a plan for tomorrow, 'kay?"

"Okay," Elizabeth answered.

Maria sprinted down the hall to drama class. Her heart felt lighter than it had in days. It was about time she took a cue from Elizabeth. Tomorrow night she wasn't going to let anything stress her out. For once she was going to kick back and enjoy her senior year. Even if it killed her.

"I've been a bad, bad girl," Jessica belted out along with the tape on her Walkman. She rolled over onto her back and cranked the volume all the way up, letting the music consume her. She'd been writing furiously in her journal and listening to her all-time favorite angstful-girl music for almost an hour.

"And it's a sad, sad world," Jessica intoned. Over

the music she thought she heard the muffled sound of a door closing. She switched off her Walkman, her ears ringing, and listened closely. Through the wall she could hear Lila moving around in her bedroom. She must have just come home.

Jessica slammed her notebook shut and pulled off her headphones. Lila had disappeared right after pretryout cheerleading practice this afternoon, and Jessica had been waiting for her to show at the house ever since.

"Have a nice lunch today, Li?" Jessica asked pointedly as she opened the door of Lila's bedroom.

"Jeez, Jess, don't you ever knock?" Lila spun around on the stool in front of her vanity mirror. She held an eye-makeup wand in one hand and a compact in the other. "I almost ended up with eye shadow out to my ear. That's a little more eighties retro than I'm prepared to go."

"How could you do that to me?" Jessica fumed.

Lila reached over and calmly placed her makeup on the vanity. She swiveled around again to face Jessica and adopted the just-this-side-of-condescending smirk that always made Jessica's skin crawl.

"What was I supposed to do?" Lila asked. "Get up and walk away?"

"Yes!" Jessica threw up her arms. Wasn't it obvious?

"Why, Jess?" Lila asked.

Jessica's blood boiled, and she had a sudden

mental picture of her body blasting through the ceiling of Lila's bedroom. "You have to be kidding me!" she yelled. "Melissa's got everyone talking behind my back, she and her stupid boyfriend have turned all the guys against me, you said yourself that she's practically got a lock on captain, and now she's trying to steal my best friend!"

Lila shook her head and turned back to her mirror. "Could you be any more melodramatic?"

Jessica felt like she'd been slapped. She and Lila had always had the kind of friendship that allowed them to be totally, sometimes brutally, honest. But after everything that had happened to her, she couldn't believe that Lila was treating her like a whining child.

"You are so transparent," Jessica said, seething.

"What's that supposed to mean?" Lila asked, glancing at Jessica in the mirror.

Her calm was too infuriating. "It means . . ." Jessica paused. "It means that you're psyched to be hanging around with Melissa. You're kissing her butt because you think she'll help make you more popular."

Lila jumped up from her stool and spun around. "What!"

Jessica took a step back. The spiteful look on Lila's face told her to back down, but she couldn't. "You said it yourself. Everyone loves Melissa, right? You just want to get popular by association."

"Get out of my room," Lila spat. Jessica felt the color drain from her cheeks. Lila sounded like she was delivering an executive order.

"Lila, I—"

"Get out, Jess," she said, more resigned. "Just get away from me."

Jessica turned slowly and headed for the door. Her hand was already on the doorknob when she turned around. Lila was just staring at her reflection in the mirror, looking like she'd had the wind knocked out of her.

Lila Fowler

Jessica and I have always had our ups and downs, but we've never been awkward and tense like this—like strangers. We've always had the same group of friends, always fought over the same guys, always exchanged clothes and magazines. But now I don't even know what to say to her. It's like I made this choice to hang out with Melissa and her friends, and now I have to completely cut myself off from the person who's been my best friend since second grade. I'm not saying I don't feel guilty for hanging out with Melissa. I do. You have no idea how much. But sometimes I'm actually happy about it. And I know I sound like a bitch, but sometimes I even feel proud.

Because I can't remember the last time someone, anyone, looked at me and Jessica . . . and chose me.

CHAPTER 7
Avoiding Human Contact

Maria felt beads of sweat spring up on her skin as soon as she entered the large warehouse space that housed the Riot on Thursday evening. The air inside was thick with cigarette smoke and a good fifteen degrees warmer than the balmy weather outside. Except for the staccato pulse of colored strobes over the dance floor, the lights were low, and it took her a moment to get her bearings.

Quick flashes of light illuminated the dance floor that stretched across the large, cavernous space. The throng of gyrating bodies was so dense that it appeared to be one sprawling mass of flailing limbs. Maria caught sporadic glimpses of flushed, glistening faces and whirling manes of hair, but she didn't recognize anyone she knew.

"Well, here goes," she muttered, diving into the crowd. She threw a couple of elbows and started searching for Elizabeth and her friends.

After having her foot mashed and her hair pulled and narrowly avoiding a guy whose drink was teetering on a collision course with her white blouse, Maria finally found them. They were seated at a table at the back of the room, under an overhanging balcony. Elizabeth was next to Andy, and Tia was practically in the lap of a tall, muscular guy.

"Hey!" Elizabeth called out with a wave. Maria had never seen her so radiant. "Isn't this place the coolest? Pull up a seat."

"Maria, this is Angel," Tia yelled, touching the guy's chest. These two were obviously a couple.

"Hi," Angel said with a gorgeous smile.

"Hi." Maria was slightly breathless from her grueling trek across the floor, but she still had the presence of mind to notice how *f-i-n-e* Angel was. She dragged an empty chair over from an adjacent table and sat down next to him and Tia. "So, what's up?"

"We were just people watching," Andy explained, nodding in the direction of the dance floor. He leaned across the table to be heard. "Check out that guy who thinks he's a one-man disco inferno. He looks like he's trying to chew and swallow his lower lip."

Maria squinted in the direction of the dance floor.

"And those freshman chicks over there might as well have *trying too hard* stamped on their foreheads," Tia added. "I mean, does that one girl really think she can pull off a minidress the size of a headband?"

"No kidding," Elizabeth agreed. "It just screams *desperate.*"

"Go easy on them, baby. They're only, like,

fourteen." Angel twirled one of Tia's many curls around his finger. "You know, I seem to remember that during freshman year, someone at this table got booted from class for wearing a very skimpy—"

"Another word and you're a dead man." Tia leaned back against Angel's chest and held a warning finger in front of his lips.

Maria took note of Tia's red-patterned wrap dress, which was sexy without being slutty, and suddenly felt scruffy and unattractive in her vintage camisole and jeans. Even Elizabeth was wearing a spaghetti-strap green tank top and a black skirt that was slit up to the knee. *Daring by Liz's standards,* Maria observed.

"You look nice," she offered reluctantly, gesturing at Elizabeth's outfit. "Did you get those at the mall the other day too?"

"Yeah, thanks." Elizabeth turned to Tia with a conspiratorial grin. "Remember that salesgirl? Could you believe that?"

"Oh my God, no." Tia put up her palm. "She was dishing attitude with a shovel."

"I think all mall employees have to undergo rigorous training sessions to perfect the art of making other people feel unworthy," Andy said.

Maria forced a smile. She was beginning to feel unworthy herself. She glanced back and forth between Elizabeth, Tia, and Andy, waiting for one of them to explain what exactly the attitudinal salesgirl had done. But they seemed to have all but forgotten Maria was at the table.

"Seriously!" Tia exclaimed. "And did you get a load of her ensemble? I mean, that was beyond fashion victim. Someone should set up a disaster-relief fund to help her."

"Oh, and did you see the way she talked to that . . ." Elizabeth turned her head slightly to address Andy, and the rest of her words were lost in the din of the crowd. Maria leaned forward, straining to hear, but she couldn't make out anything over the pulsing bass line of the music. Tia obviously heard since she threw back her head and laughed.

Andy shook his head, grinning. "Harsh, but true."

Harsh? Elizabeth "Butter-wouldn't-melt-in-my-mouth" Wakefield had been harsh? Did these strangers suddenly know Liz better than she did?

Tia was leaning forward, saying something animated that Maria couldn't hear over the music. Angel turned to Maria. "So," he said in the booming tone of someone who has designated himself responsible for making polite conversation with an outcast. "You're a senior too?"

Maria smiled tightly as they ran through the basic generic-conversation points. Yes, she was a senior. Yes, she had thought about colleges. Wow, he was going to Stanford, congratulations. No, her house hadn't been hit in the quake, thank God. Neither had his. She was grateful that he'd picked up on her discomfort and made an effort to make her feel welcome, but he shouldn't have had to. It was a sad thing when a total stranger could read her better than her best friend.

"Angel, you've gotta hear this!" Tia cried, tugging at his sleeve. "Liz, tell him what you just told us."

Abruptly Maria stood up. "I'm going to go get something to drink." She trained her eyes on Elizabeth, hoping she would offer to come along. "Does anyone want anything?"

"No, thanks." Elizabeth shook her head casually, oblivious to Maria's mood.

Maria's whole body was rigid with annoyance as she made her way through the crowd. Didn't Elizabeth realize she was completely ignoring her?

She walked around the perimeter of the dance floor and found a narrow spiral staircase leading up. She stood back and saw that the upstairs balcony was almost an entire second floor. It looked like there was a bar up there.

Maria slowly threaded her way up the stairs. She stepped aside to avoid a couple of big, meaty-necked guys who were obviously racing down and collided with a girl in a strapless dress, who shot her a withering look.

By the time she reached the second floor, she felt like she'd been through gym class. She was all sweaty again, and her throat felt scratchy from the smoke. She wondered if some people just weren't cut out for having fun.

Maybe she should haul her sorry butt back home. But just as Maria was about to call her social life quits, someone caught her eye. She fought to restrain the grin that was twitching at the corners of her mouth.

Sitting on a corner stool at the bar, looking even more perfect than usual, was Conner McDermott. And he was smiling at her.

Conner took a sip of Coke and glanced at his watch. The blaring, bass-heavy electronic music jabbed steadily at his temples like a dulled ice pick. Lame. Across the bar a cluster of scantily clad freshman girls were blatantly making eyes at him, then giggling and shushing each other in a desperate attempt to act cool and suave. They were obviously members of the yearly crop of geeks who swarmed into the Riot all psyched to have "discovered" the place. Lame, lame, lame.

Normally Conner would be downstairs with his friends, listening to Tia give her little fashion-police reports and Andy keep up his blow-by-blow commentary on the dancing fools (never mind that Andy himself was the worst dancer Conner had ever seen). In fact, that was what he had come here to do. But moments after he had arrived, he'd seen that they were sitting with Elizabeth. The girl was invading his life. First his classes, then his house, and now his friends. Was nothing sacred?

He might have gone down there anyway just to prove he wasn't affected, but he'd had to physically restrain himself from reaching out and touching Elizabeth's smooth, tan skin more than once over the past few days. He didn't trust his behavior not to reveal anything.

He considered just downing the rest of his soda and taking off, but that might mean facing his mother, whom he'd been studiously avoiding since the country-club debacle. Conner ran an exasperated hand through his hair and glanced around the Riot again. His gaze lit on the stairway that led down to the main level. Maybe he could just walk out and keep on going.

Then he saw her. That gorgeous girl he'd seen in the hall the other day. She was model beautiful. Stunning tall, athletic body. Flawless milk-chocolate skin. Short black hair that exposed high, apple-round cheekbones and wide, luminous eyes.

Her whole face lit up when she spotted him. Maybe tonight wouldn't be such a depressing waste after all.

The girl moved to the bar and stood just inches away from him. The expression on her face was part expectant, part studied nonchalant.

"Hey." Conner flashed her his most charming smile.

"Hey," she said, sounding shy and a little breathless. Her gaze went to her shoes before returning to his face.

"You look familiar," he offered. "Sorry, that sounded like a line, but you really do."

She laughed—not a big laugh—but not a girlie little giggle either. "I believe you. You go to SVH, right?"

"Right," Conner confirmed. "So, what's up? Are you up here looking for someone?"

She grimaced slightly as she slid onto the stool next to him. "I just needed some fresh air. Not that this is exactly the place for it."

"I know what you mean." Conner cupped his fingers around his glass and gazed down at the flat surface of the soda. "So, are you here with your friends, or . . ." He left the question unfinished. She would fill in the blank if she needed to.

"Yeah, but I guess I'm just not really in the mood for hanging out in a big group tonight." Maria shrugged. "You know?"

"Yeah, I know." It was the truth. He knew exactly. And better yet she hadn't inserted *boyfriend,* or even *date,* in the opening he'd given her. "Sometimes the vibe downstairs just gets a little . . . oppressive."

"Exactly," she agreed. He was relieved that she didn't ask him what he meant by oppressive. "You are not looking at a social butterfly."

"I'm more into keeping a low profile myself." He was surprised to find himself actually sympathizing with her. No prepackaged lines needed. "But for the record, my name's Conner."

"Maria." She hesitated for a second before continuing. "Actually, I kind of know who you are. My friend Elizabeth is staying with you." She quickly turned to flag down the bartender. "A Coke, please?"

Conner digested this information. Apparently there was just no escaping Elizabeth. Girls sometimes had an "understanding" with their friends when one of them liked a guy. It was a weird little code of honor he'd encountered before. If he hooked up with Maria, Elizabeth might freak out. She seemed like exactly the kind of girl who would create a lot of drama over something like that.

But it wasn't his problem. He didn't have a relationship going with Elizabeth, not even a platonic one. He had better things to do than worry about what she thought or how she felt. And wasn't Elizabeth the one who was downstairs hanging out with *his* friends?

Besides, the girl had ordered a Coke instead of a diet Coke. That was reason enough to get to know her.

Maria was looking at him directly, with interest. Not darting her eyes all around or fawning. She didn't giggle hysterically or blush or constantly put her hand on his knee like most girls did. And she could actually carry on a conversation that wasn't of the what-classes-are-you-taking variety. Maria had definite possibilities.

The bartender set a Coke in front of Maria. "One-fifty."

Maria's hand went to her back jeans pocket, but Conner quickly flipped a couple of bills on the bar. "I've got it."

Maria looked surprised. "Are you sure? I mean, I can—"

Conner waved her aside. "That's okay." He met her eyes and dropped his voice slightly. "You can get me next time."

You can get me next time. The words chimed sweetly in Maria's head.

"Thanks." It took all of Maria's self-control to sound casual. There was an infinite array of possibilities in *next time.*

Conner lifted his glass. "Anyway, here's to avoiding human contact. Well . . ." He clinked it with hers. "Maybe not *all* human contact."

Maria was trying so hard to keep her cool, her knees were shaking. But so far, he didn't seem to notice.

She set her glass down on the bar and made eye contact that she hoped was warm but not too eager. *Stay calm,* she ordered herself. No need to get all worked up. He wasn't the hottest guy she'd ever seen or anything. Right.

"So how come you're not hanging with your friends?" Conner asked. "Most people come to this place to see and be seen."

Maria shrugged. "I guess I just think being part of a whole big 'scene' is overrated," she said carefully. Well, it sounded better than admitting she spent most of her time in her room, studying. "I used to do some acting when I was a kid, so I know how messed up people get when they just live for attention."

Conner raised his eyebrows. "An actress, huh?"

"Yeah, I was in a couple of movies, TV specials, that kind of stuff." *Shut up, Maria,* a tiny voice nagged. Her face grew hot. She sounded like a desperate has-been clinging pathetically to her past feeble glories. "Peaked at twelve, washed up at thirteen."

"Wait a second," Conner said, his green eyes sparkling. "Weren't you in that movie about the kids who save the Christmas elf?"

"Get out. You do *not* remember that," Maria said, embarrassed and pleased at once.

Conner nodded, grinning. God, he was perfect. "Are you kidding? My sister is fifteen years old, and she still makes me watch it every year."

"I'm so sorry!" Maria laughed. "I've been a party to your annual torture. I'll completely understand if you want to walk away now."

"I won't be doing that," Conner said solemnly. Maria blushed from scalp to toes. "You've obviously avoided the curse."

98

"Curse?" Maria repeated blankly.

"Most of those cute telegenic kids end up going through an awkward phase that they just can't come out of. Trolls for life." Conner's eyes crinkled adorably when he smiled.

"Thanks for the vote of confidence." Okay, so she was a nontroll. That was a good thing. "So, why are *you* playing keep away from the crowd?"

Conner turned away and took a long, slow sip of his drink. Maria actually *felt* a chill and knew she'd crossed some line. An eternity seemed to pass. Maria was about to slink away when a slow song came on.

"Finally," Conner said, placing his glass directly on top of the water ring it had already made on the bar. "I was getting sick of all the techno they've been playing."

Maria felt her lungs constrict, and the words hissed out quickly, like air escaping from a cut tire. "Doyouwannadance?"

To her surprise, he seemed unfazed by the profound depths of her dorkiness. His eyes held hers for a second before he responded. "Sure."

Maria followed him downstairs to the dance floor, taking the opportunity to wipe her clammy hands on her jeans. No point in icking him out now.

But when Conner slipped his strong arms around her waist, pressing her close to him, all her anxiety melted away. She wrapped her arms around his neck, and suddenly it was like the last piece of a puzzle had snapped into place. Everything just felt right.

Conner leaned forward slightly. His breath was soft on her face.

Maria couldn't believe this funny, sweet, gorgeous guy was actually dancing with her. Her. Maria Slater, crown geek of the Western world. But the gently firm pressure of his arms around her, his chest fitted snug against hers, was undeniably real.

Maria tilted her head back to gaze into Conner's eyes. He wasn't smiling now. He fixed her with an intense, searching look that made her feel like he'd known her in a past life.

Slowly he lowered his face toward hers. The room seemed to whirl around them in a blur. Gently, so gently, he brushed her lips with his. For a long, charged moment his face hovered millimeters away. Then his mouth pressed to Maria's for a soft, deep, searing kiss that spread fire through her whole body.

When Conner broke away from her a moment later, Maria's eyes fluttered open. After a beat she resumed breathing.

"Come with me," he whispered. "I know where we can get some of that fresh air you were looking for."

Maria took the hand he offered and let him lead her off the dance floor, back up the stairs. Her heart was thudding wildly in her chest. She wasn't in the habit of kissing guys she'd just met.

But then, it wasn't every day she met a guy like Conner McDermott. As nervous as she might be, the idea of not following him was unthinkable.

Jessica Wakefield

I knew this girl in middle school who used to make fun of everybody. She picked on people's clothes, on their parents, on their friends, on their hair. She walked around with her nose so high in the air, it was scraping the ceiling. And she had this way of looking at people — just looking at them — and making them feel like they weren't worthy to be in her presence. Like they would never be worthy.

She was loud and obnoxious and egotistical, and everyone was afraid of her. Even her best friends, including me, were afraid of her. You never knew who she was going to turn on next. Who she would publicly humiliate simply because they'd chosen to wear the same color as she had that morning.

But you know what? I miss her. Because at least with Janet you knew where you stood. She was kind enough to be blatant and face you head-on. So you weren't always looking over your shoulder, wondering what was going to happen next.

CHAPTER

Complications

After several hours, being incessantly stabbed with red lights felt a little like being in hell. Elizabeth glanced at her watch, then gazed out at the dance floor with smoke-stung eyes. She was beginning to get irritated. Last night on the phone Maria had offered her a ride home, and they'd agreed that if they split up, they would meet at the door at eleven. Now it was almost eleven-thirty. Tia, Angel, and Andy had left half an hour ago. Elizabeth had enjoyed hanging out with them, but now her feet ached from dancing in pumps, and her throat hurt from yelling herself hoarse.

Elizabeth scanned the crowd again, shielding her eyes with her hand to block the blinding strobe lights. The mob on the dance floor had thinned out, but not by much. The only people she recognized were Lila Fowler and Amy Sutton. They were talking to a wispy girl with dark chestnut hair and a short-haired, trendily dressed Asian American girl.

Elizabeth wondered why Jessica wasn't with them. Her twin never missed a night out, especially when Lila was involved. Those two were constantly trying to one-up each other socially. But right now she didn't really care what her sister was up to. All she wanted was to get home, peel out of her reeking clothes, and curl up in her bed.

Finally Maria emerged from the crowd and practically skipped across the floor. As she got closer, Elizabeth could see that her hair was all messed up and the dark lipstick she'd been wearing earlier had completely disappeared. The girl was aglow—big time.

"Liz! There you are!" Maria exclaimed, sounding unnaturally delighted. "I'm so sorry I lost track of time, but I have *such* a story for you!"

"What?" Elizabeth asked warily as they left the club. Something about Maria's tone was causing stomach knots. She sounded like a girl who had just hooked up. And that wasn't a Maria type of thing to do.

Outside the Riot the clean, cool night air was a welcome relief. As they headed across the parking lot, Maria hugged her arms to her chest and let out an enormous, contented sigh. The stomach knots tightened.

"Liz, you're never going to believe this," Maria declared in a giddy voice that only vaguely resembled her own. "Guess who I ran into?" Double knots.

Maria was bouncing on the balls of her feet like a Ping-Pong ball on too much caffeine. And in the last few days she'd only expressed interest in one person. . . .

"Who?" Elizabeth asked apprehensively.

"Conner!" Maria exclaimed, grabbing Elizabeth's wrists. "Can you believe it?"

Elizabeth felt faint. "That's . . ." There wasn't a word in the English language that could have completed that sentence for Elizabeth. She wrested herself from Maria's grasp and rushed over to the Slaters' green Taurus. Maria bent to unlock her door, then got in and leaned across the seat to unlock Elizabeth's side.

"Are you okay?" Maria asked. "Don't you want to hear what happened?"

I'd rather hear you recite the Iliad *in pig Latin,* Elizabeth thought. "Sure," she muttered.

"Okay, I met Conner up at the bar," Maria said, starting the engine. "We started talking, and—Liz, have you ever been up to the roof of the Riot?"

"No," Elizabeth said flatly. There was something intimate about the way Maria said Conner's name. Something possessive. She trained her eyes on the road ahead, unable to look at Maria. The knots were having a dance party. Elizabeth had intended to keep Maria away from Conner, and instead they had only met because Elizabeth had invited Maria out tonight. The irony wasn't lost on her. "Take the next right," she directed.

Maria steered the car onto Myrtle Avenue.

"Well, it's unbelievable. At least it was for me."
Maria giggled. "The view is amazing. It's like you
can see all of Sweet Valley. And all the stars . . . It's
incredible."

"Incredible," Elizabeth echoed hollowly. "Huh."

They reached a stoplight, and Maria turned to
look at Elizabeth. "Listen, Liz, I know you don't
like Conner," she said. "But I bet if you got to
know him, you'd think he was totally cool. I mean,
he was so sweet to me."

"Sweet?" Conner?

"We talked for a while," Maria continued, "and
then he asked me to dance, and then . . ." She sighed
again. "He kissed me, Liz, and boy, can he kiss."

Elizabeth rested her hand on the door handle,
feeling like she might throw up. Apparently the
knots wanted to take the party outside. She turned
her face toward the window so Maria wouldn't see
the tears that had sprung to her eyes. She wished
she could be happy for Maria, but she'd lost control of her emotions. She hated her own weakness.
The Sandborns' white house glowed in the distance up ahead. Just a few more minutes and she
would be out of this nightmare.

"I mean, at first I was kind of nervous. It was
like everything was happening so fast." Maria was
oblivious. "But once he kissed me . . . I swear, I've
never experienced anything even remotely like that
in my life. It was like . . . magical." Maria giggled

again. "God, I sound like a giant cheeseball. But I don't know how else to describe it. Nobody's ever kissed me like that."

"That's great, Maria. Really." Elizabeth didn't think she could stand to be in the car a single second longer. Every one of Maria's dreamy details was like a butcher knife through her heart.

Maria slowed the car to a stop and gazed up at the white gables of Conner's house. "So this is where he lives," she said wistfully.

Elizabeth was about to hurl. Frantically she fumbled with the door handle and climbed out of the car. A moment later she was standing on the sidewalk.

"I—I'm sorry, Maria, I just don't feel well all of a sudden," she said lamely. "I'll see you tomorrow."

Elizabeth turned and ran toward the house, praying that she could somehow wipe the image of Maria's excited face, the sound of her hopeful words, the image of Maria and Conner lip to lip, from her memory forever.

Angel pulled the car up in front of Tia's white-stucco ranch house and leaned over to give her their usual old-married-couple good-bye kiss. When he drew back, Tia found herself grabbing the lapels of his jacket and pulling him toward her. She kissed him almost fiercely, trying to memorize the way his lips felt on hers, the scent of his cologne, the soft pressure of his palms on her back. She couldn't help wondering how many kisses they had left.

"What was that for?" he asked, his breath shallow, when she finally let him go.

She could tell him—tell him she didn't want him to go. But then it would hang like a weight over their time together. It wasn't fair to make him feel guilty about getting on with his life.

"Can't a girl kiss her boyfriend?" she asked instead, smiling coyly.

"I didn't say I was complaining." Angel tucked a stray lock of hair behind her ear. "Okay, Tia. Sweet dreams. I'll talk to you tomorrow."

"Get home safe." Tia got out of the car and closed the door, then leaned through the open window. "Love you," she said.

"Love you too." He kissed two fingertips and touched them gently to her lips.

Tia took one last look at Angel's face, then willed herself not to glance over her shoulder as she scampered up the walkway to her house.

She tiptoed down the darkened hall, past her little brothers' room. Inside her bedroom she closed the door and changed into a T-shirt and boxers. Then she slipped through the kitchen and out the back door onto the small brick patio. It was her sanctuary, the place where she came when she needed to clear her head. Her problems always seemed small and fleeting under the stars.

She didn't expect to see Conner sitting there.

"Hey," he said. His back was to her, but he must have heard her approach.

"Hey." Tia sat down next to him on the weather-beaten welcome mat that lay across the bricks. "To what do I owe the honor of this visit?" She hugged her knees to her chest and tilted her head back to drink in the night air.

Conner simply shrugged and kept staring straight ahead.

Tia decided to take a different approach. "You didn't show tonight."

"Yeah." This was going nowhere fast. If she wanted to find out what he was doing here, she'd have to give stoic boy a jolt.

"It's Elizabeth, isn't it?" she asked, fixing her eyes on his profile.

Conner turned to her, his eyes blazing. "Why is it always about Elizabeth? Can't I have one single moment without her name coming up?"

Score ten points for Tia. "Sorry!" she said. "I had no idea you were so . . . emotional about her."

"I'm not emotional," Conner said, turning forward again. "It's just . . . Isn't there something else we can talk about?"

Tia decided to back off. There was definitely something going on between Conner and Elizabeth. Maybe nothing had actually *happened* yet, but they were either a sordid affair or a ten-round fight waiting to happen. Either way, Tia knew better than to press Conner on the issue. He'd tell her what she needed to know when the time was right.

"What do you think's gonna happen when Angel leaves for school?" Tia asked.

Conner glanced at her, and she could tell he was minorly intrigued. "Whaddaya mean?"

Tia pulled her knees in tighter as a light breeze skittered across the yard. "I mean, do you think he'll forget about me?"

Conner actually laughed. "Are you kidding me? Tia, if there is only one thing I'm sure about in this world, it's that you and Angel will be together forever. I'm planning on carrying your kids around on my back one day."

Tia smirked at the mental picture. "Yeah, but there's all that distance. . . ."

Conner's eyebrows came together. "Wait a minute," he said, sliding himself around and facing her fully. "You're not thinking of breaking up with the guy because he's going to Stanford, are you?"

"Well, when you put it that way—"

"Tee, that distance doesn't have to mean anything if you don't let it," Conner said. "You and Angel—" He paused and looked up at the sky. "I don't know—you're so close. You're like the only people I've ever known who actually love each other like you're supposed to." He turned his face toward her, and his earnest expression took Tia by surprise.

She'd only seen it a few times in her life. Conner usually avoided touchy-feely stuff at all costs. "For you two the distance won't matter."

He picked up a tiny stick and started mashing it against the ground. Tia took a deep breath and stared across the yard at the swing set she and Conner used to play on when they were little. She smiled wistfully. From contests over who could swing the highest to deep conversations on love.

"Thanks, Conner." Tia stood up and dusted the dirt from the back of her shorts. "You're probably right."

"I know I'm right, Tee." He stood and looked her directly in the eyes. "I'm not the love expert—" Tia laughed, and Conner allowed a small smile. "But you and Angel will get through this."

"Thanks." Tia reached up and hugged him, and Conner wrapped his arms around her waist. They held each other tightly, and Tia couldn't help wondering if Conner needed a hug even more than she did.

"I'll see you tomorrow," Conner said when they parted. "It'll be okay." He turned and cut across her lawn and through the line of trees, heading for their secret shortcut.

"I wish I could be so sure," Tia whispered as she watched his shadowed form.

She and Angel might be the perfect couple, but that wasn't the point. The point was, Tia needed to

take control of the situation, act instead of just react-
ing. She couldn't handle being little-girl-left-behind,
always pining for her boyfriend, clinging desperately
to a long-distance relationship. Everyone knew those
never worked out. The distance just made the relationship more like an obligation than a pleasure. The
thought she'd been working so hard to smother was
steadily rising to the surface of her mind.

If she was strong enough, if she fought every
sentimental bone in her body, she could save herself from being left behind in lonely limbo.

Dear Diary,

I know this is insane, but ever since
Monday afternoon I haven't been able to stop
thinking about one little thing.

Will.

What was he going to say to me before I
walked into math class? Did he know what
they'd written on the board? Was he going to
warn me? Was he going to apologize? Or . . .

and I know this sounds like a product of my overactive imagination . . . but maybe he was stalling so they would have time to write it. Maybe he had even <u>told</u> them to do it.

Part of me wants to call him so badly. Just call him and ask him why he's doing this to me. Or at least why he's letting the rest of them do this to me. But there are a few reasons why I can't.

1. I would feel so pathetic;

2. I doubt he would even be honest with me. He hasn't told the truth yet, as far as I can tell; and

3. I have a feeling I already know the reason. He's doing it for Melissa. Which just makes <u>him</u> pathetic.

"Hey, girlfriend!" Tia sang out, bounding onto the counter stool next to Elizabeth's at House of Java.

It was Friday morning, and after the previous night's festivities Elizabeth felt the need for some serious pre-homeroom caffeine. "Hook me up with an iced hazelnut," Tia said to the woman behind the counter. "Someone's in a good mood today." Elizabeth laughed as Ally, her manager, poured iced coffee into a tall glass for Tia. "God, where do you get all this energy? I'm a waste of space after last night."

"Cheerleading tryouts are this afternoon, so I have to start being . . . cheerful. Or something," Tia answered.

Elizabeth grinned as Ally set down the iced coffee in front of Tia. "I keep forgetting that I'm actually friends with a cheerleader—," Elizabeth began.

"If the words *perky* or *ditzy* come out of your mouth, I'm going to dump this pitcher of half-and-half over your head," Tia warned.

"Don't worry," Elizabeth said, sipping her coffee. "After many heated debates with my sister, I now understand that cheerleading is, what's the word? Oh, yeah, *empowering*."

Tia chuckled as she pinched four packets of sugar together and waved them from side to side. "I'd say that's pretty accurate."

Elizabeth's smile faded. "Tia, can I ask you something? You know what's going on with Jess, right?"

Tia nodded, her face serious. "I felt weird bringing it up to you, but yeah, I've seen what Melissa Fox and her friends are doing. It's really

114

messed up. But that's just how Melissa is. It's like she has this sinister territory-marking instinct."

Elizabeth sighed and rested her elbows on the counter. "I told Jessica it had to blow over eventually, but she just seems so tense all the time."

"Don't worry," Tia said. "Melissa's pulled this kind of stuff before. Eventually people just get sick of the whole 'she can't play on my team' vibe, you know?"

"I guess," Elizabeth answered pensively. "It's just Jessica has this habit of making the worst of a bad situation and—"

"I totally understand, but I'm sure Jessica can take care of herself, Aunt Elizabeth." Tia smirked. "Besides, not all of us El Carro people are pure evil. You had fun hanging out with us last night, didn't you?"

"Yeah, it was great," Elizabeth said, more brightly than she actually felt. Elizabeth *so* wanted to ask Tia if Conner had said anything about Maria. She was afraid her question would betray her own feelings, but ultimately Elizabeth couldn't resist. "Not as much fun as *some* people, though," she said in what she hoped was an incidental coffee-chat voice.

Tia leaned one elbow on the counter and turned to face Elizabeth completely. "Do I smell gossip? Spill!"

Elizabeth shifted her weight and placed her cup on the counter. "Well," she said, trying to mimic Jessica's gossip-hound voice. "Maria kind of hooked up with somebody."

115

"She did?" Tia gasped. "Good for her! I wondered where she ran off to. Who was it? Anybody I know?"

"Yeah, actually." Elizabeth took a deep breath. "It was Conner."

"Oh!" Tia's face fell, and the grin fell with it.

"What? What is it?" Elizabeth pressed, as casually as she could. Her whole body was tense.

Tia took a sip of iced coffee before replying. "I probably shouldn't say anything. I don't want to stress your friend out for no reason."

"You can tell me," Elizabeth insisted, applying a death grip to a paper napkin. She was about to burst. Did she sound as hysterical as she felt? Carefully she added, "I mean, Maria's my best friend. I don't want her to get hurt."

Tia swirled her straw in her coffee. "Well," she said slowly, "when it comes to girls, Conner is kind of a bad scene. When he starts seeing someone, it's like there's an expiration date, you know?" She took another sip of coffee. "The second it starts getting serious, he kind of shuts down. At least, that's how it seems to me. He doesn't really like to talk about relationship stuff. But I know a few girls who say they got burned."

"Wow." Elizabeth dropped the torn napkin on the counter, struggling to absorb this new information. Of course, it meant her original opinion of Conner was right.

Then he and Maria won't last, Elizabeth thought.

"Don't get me wrong," Tia added, looking almost apologetic. "I mean, Conner's one of my best friends. He just doesn't know the first thing about the whole love deal."

Elizabeth figured she had one question left before Tia started to suspect an ulterior motive. "So why do you think he's so weird with girls he's interested in?"

"That's a tough one." Tia wiped her mouth on the back of her hand and gazed at the counter for a minute. "Let's put it this way. Conner is . . . complicated."

Complicated? Great. Elizabeth was glad Tia wasn't being vague or anything.

"Listen, don't say anything to Maria, okay?" Tia flashed another dimpled grin. "Let the crazy kids have their fun. The start of the romance is always the best part—not that I can remember that far back." Her smile wattage dropped a notch.

After a second she tossed a couple of bills on the counter and hopped off her stool. "Well, now that I'm artificially stimulated, I want to get in a little practice time before school. Soon I will become one of the few, the proud, the pom-pom chicks." She shouldered her gym bag.

"Good luck." Elizabeth watched Tia stride out, the new info on Conner still processing in her mind.

Complicated. That could mean anything. Maybe she *should* warn Maria off Conner. But if

117

she did that, she'd have to practice what she preached. As much as she hated the idea of missing out on chance, midnight kitchen encounters, Elizabeth was going to have to start keeping to herself in the house. There was no way she could get involved with Conner in any sense of the word now that he and Maria had something going.

It was time to put this stupid crush behind her.

TIA RAMIREZ

DEAR ANGEL,

AS I WRITE THIS, YOU'RE PROBABLY GETTING READY FOR BED, A FEW BLOCKS AWAY. BUT BY THE TIME YOU READ THIS, YOU'LL BE AT COLLEGE, DOING WHO KNOWS WHAT. YOU BETTER NOT BE AT SOME CHUG-FEST KEGGER OR HANGING OUT IN THE BASEMENT OF SOME FRAT HOUSE WITH A BUNCH OF THICK-NECKED GREEKS URGING YOU TO DO UNSPEAKABLE THINGS TO SHEEP.

WHAT MATTERS IS, YOU'RE NOT HERE. I CAN'T SEE YOU OR TOUCH YOU OR SMELL YOU OR KISS YOU. I CAN'T JUST CALL YOU UP AND KNOW YOU'LL BE OVER IN FIVE MINUTES IF I FAIL A TEST OR HAVE A FIGHT WITH MY PARENTS OR CRAVE BEN &

JERRY'S. JUST THINKING ABOUT IT,
I MISS YOU ALREADY.

THIS IS SO HARD. WHAT I'M
TRYING TO SAY IS . . . I DON'T
THINK I CAN STAND NEEDING
YOU SO MUCH AND KNOWING
YOU'RE NOT HERE. BUT IT'S
IMPOSSIBLE TO ADMIT IT OUT
LOUD, WHEN MY MOTHER'S
ALWAYS GOING ON ABOUT WHAT
A WONDERFUL YOUNG MAN YOU
ARE, AND MY LITTLE BROTHERS
CONSTANTLY ASK ME WHEN
YOU'RE TAKING THEM HIKING
AGAIN, AND ANDY AND CONNER
TALK ABOUT THE TWO OF US
LIKE WE WERE SOME MUTANT,
JOINED-AT-THE-HIP FREAK OF
NATURE. NOT TO MENTION THAT
WHEN I LOOK IN YOUR EYES, I
CAN'T IMAGINE EVER BEING
APART FROM YOU. . . .

SEE, HERE I GO WITH THE

HALLMARK STUFF AGAIN. WHAT I'M <u>TRYING</u> TO SAY IS:

ANGEL, IT'S TOO HARD FOR ME TO TELL YOU THIS RIGHT NOW, BUT ONCE YOU'RE AT SCHOOL, I DON'T THINK WE SHOULD SEE EACH OTHER ANYMORE.

THERE. I SAID IT.

OH, WHO AM I KIDDING? I CAN'T DO THIS TO HIM IN A LETTER. I OWE IT TO HIM TO SAY IT TO HIS FACE.

AND I WILL. AS SOON AS I GET UP THE NERVE.

CHAPTER 9
On the Edge

Jessica hit the play button on her Walkman and raised her arms over her head. After a second a driving rock beat surged through her headphones, and she launched into her carefully choreographed series of steps. Cheerleading tryouts were this afternoon, and it was tradition for the squad hopefuls to gather in the courtyard during lunch for one last run-through. Jessica had her cheer down cold, but she wanted to make sure her dance sequence was up to par.

Peripherally she saw Amy Sutton tumble from a handstand into a heap on the ground. Through her headphones Jessica heard Amy burst into laughter and screech, "Omigod, did you guys *see* that?"

Distracted, Jessica missed a step and halted in her tracks. She hit stop and rewind and stood, feeling suddenly self-conscious. Did she look like a huge geek jumping around all by herself in the middle of the SVH courtyard?

Everyone else was running through their routines too, but they were standing in a pack fifty feet away. It would have made her feel so much better to be over there exchanging last-minute pointers with Lila and Amy and Annie. But she wasn't about to go up and rub shoulders with Melissa Fox, so she'd told everyone she wanted some time to herself so she could concentrate.

Jessica leaned against the courtyard wall and took a swig from her water bottle. It was a gorgeous day, the kind that usually reminded her she'd rather live in southern California than anywhere else on earth. The sun beat down from a sky so clear that the world seemed to be in sharper focus than usual. All around her small clusters of students sat perched on the wall or sprawled on the lawn, laughing and gossiping. The chants and claps of the cheerleader wanna-bes floated through the air. From across the lawn a hip-hop beat pulsed from someone's radio.

Nobody was talking to Jessica or even seemed to notice her presence. She might as well be a band geek.

"Go, Gladiators!" Melissa Fox's voice shouted a few feet away.

Jessica shook herself back to reality. Self-pity wasn't getting her anywhere. She had to focus on her practice. The idea of Melissa cheering for *her* school team made Jessica all the more determined to blow the girl out of the water at tryouts.

She switched on her Walkman again and started the routine over. After a few steps Jessica felt herself loosening up and getting into it. The hyper-energetic song was a perfect choice. It always kicked her into high gear. And it set her apart from the others, who would doubtless be using all the old standby tunes.

Melissa cartwheeled into her view, a windmill blur of rail-straight limbs. Jessica lost her place, stumbled, and switched her Walkman off again. Her muscles were beginning to tense up with frustration. Melissa was trying to distract her on purpose. Jessica was sure of it.

Stay focused, she reminded herself, rewinding the tape. Making the team was a no-brainer. And with her experience she was sure to be captain again. But since cheerleading was the one good thing she had going for her, she had to make sure she was flawless.

"Melissa, that was like the best routine I've ever seen in my life," Cherie's sickening-sweet voice called out loudly over the music. "You're *so* going to make captain."

Another comment that was obviously for Jessica's benefit. Disgusted, Jessica switched her Walkman back on and kicked out, visualizing her foot planted squarely in Cherie Reese's gut. She brought her leg down too fast and had to take a few steps backward to keep her balance.

Jessica rewound her tape and popped it out of her Walkman. She might as well leave now and get changed back into her regular school clothes. She wasn't going to stick around and let Melissa and her friends try to undermine her confidence.

Jessica tossed her stuff into her duffel bag and headed around the building toward the locker room. Lila might be sure that Melissa was just an innocent cheerleading hopeful, but Jessica knew better. She was not going to let Melissa push her off the team. This was *her* squad. Once Melissa and her friends realized their little intimidation campaign wasn't working, maybe they'd ease up a little on the psychological warfare.

"Liz! Hey, Liz!"

Elizabeth stopped trying to ignore Maria's insistent whispering and turned her head slightly to the left. There was a folded piece of notepaper staring her in the face. Elizabeth grabbed it and unfolded it on her desk as Ms. Dalton droned on.

"Repétéz, s'il vous plaît. Il y a une jeune fille—"

The contents of the note made Elizabeth's stomach squeeze.

Do you know where Conner is today? I haven't been able to find him anywhere. Is he sick?

Elizabeth weighed her options for a moment. Conner had been in creative writing, so he wasn't home sick. The thought that he might be avoiding bumping into Maria was intriguing. Maybe he wasn't interested after all. Elizabeth picked up her pen and jotted a reply.

I don't know, Maria. But maybe you should be glad you can't find him.

Elizabeth heard the rustling of paper, then a pause, then the scratching of a pen. She held her hand back under the desk, and Maria placed the note in her palm.

What's that supposed to mean?

Elizabeth scrawled a response before she could really consider the consequences of what she was doing.

one of Conner's best friends told me that Conner isn't exactly the perfect guy you think he is. Every girl he goes out with ends up with her heart broken. She said his relationships have a preset shelf life. He's not

*serious about you, Maria. I'm sorry to
have to be the one to tell you.*

It was a little harsh, but it got the point across.
Elizabeth dropped the note behind her back and
tried to concentrate on the lesson instead of listening for Maria's reaction.

"*Il y'a un jeun fils—*"

The shrill clanging of Friday afternoon's final
bell pierced the air, and the sluggish last-period
classroom came to life. The rest of Ms. Dalton's
words were drowned out by the scraping of chairs
against the floor. "For Monday finish chapter
three," she shouted over the drumbeat of stam-
peding feet. "Au revoir!"

Elizabeth gathered up her French book and
notebook and stuffed them into her backpack.
Before she could even stand, Maria had brushed
past her and was rushing for the door.

"Maria!" Elizabeth called. "Wait up!" She slung her
backpack over her shoulder and chased her friend.

"Maria!"

Just outside the classroom door Maria stopped
and whirled around.

"God, Liz, are you going around trying to dig
up dirt on Conner now?" Her eyes were sharp
with anger. "I know you don't like him, but—"

"I wasn't trying to dig up anything," Elizabeth
lied. "I just—"

"How could you say that to me?" Maria interrupted. "'He's not serious about you, Maria,'" she recited in a snotty voice. "What do you know about him or about the way he feels about me?"

"I didn't . . . I mean, I don't know—"

"Right. You don't know," Maria said.

All Elizabeth could do was just stand there, choking on guilt over hurting her best friend for her own selfish motives. She'd let her fixation with Conner get way out of hand.

Maria shrugged and let her hand slap against her side in exasperation. "Look, Liz, I understand you're just trying to be a good friend," she said, backing away. "But this is my call. I mean, even if that stuff about Conner is true, who's to say he can't change? Why can't you consider the possibility that maybe he really cares about me? That I could be the one who changes all that for him?"

Elizabeth's heart twisted. She stared openmouthed at Maria, unable to find the words to respond. *Because I want to be that girl, that's why!*

Maria looked expectantly at Elizabeth for a long minute, then shook her head in disgust or disbelief, Elizabeth couldn't tell. "Whatever, Liz. I'll talk to you later. Right now I'm going to go call Conner."

Maria strode off down the hall, leaving Elizabeth to gape after her.

Elizabeth had always thought that figuring out the right thing to do was the hard part. Once you knew what it was, you just did it. But whenever Conner was concerned, it seemed like she had a bizarre compulsion to do the opposite of whatever she thought was right. It made no sense at all.

"Excellent work, Wakefield." Coach Laufeld tucked her clipboard under her arm. "Take five, then come back here and set up for your dance."

Jessica's muscles were still trembling from the effort she'd put into her cheer, but as she jogged to the locker room, she was buoyed by adrenaline. She'd executed her cheer perfectly. Jessica had almost forgotten what it was like to feel good about something. Now all she had to do was nail the dance sequence, which would be cake after all her practice.

She hurried to the bench where she'd dumped her stuff and started rifling through her duffel bag. Extracting a towel, she mopped the sweat from her face. She tugged on her black spandex unitard in all the spots that needed tugging, then rummaged around the bottom of the bag, feeling for her dance tape.

It wasn't there.

Instantly the adrenaline rushing through Jessica's veins switched from the happy kind to the panic kind. She dumped out the contents of her duffel and dropped to her knees, frantically pawing through scrunchies and spritzers and sweatpants. The tape wasn't there.

Jessica shoved everything back into her bag and raced back out to the football field. "Lila!" she panted as she reached the bleachers. "*Lila!*"

After a second Lila leaned over the railing. "What, Jess?"

Jessica tilted her head back to look up at her friend. "I can't find my tape anywhere! I don't understand what could have happened to it! What am I going to do?"

Lila stared down at Jessica, and for a second she looked almost sad.

"It's got to be there somewhere," she said in a calm, reasonable voice.

"But it's not," Jessica hissed. "I looked everywhere." She felt herself teetering dangerously on the edge of a breakdown. She couldn't lose it. Not now.

"Jessica, just calm down, go back, and check one more time," Lila said soothingly. "It has to be there."

Jessica took a deep breath. "You're right. I must've just been so stressed out that I didn't see it. It was probably staring me right in the face."

Jessica sprinted back to the locker room and searched through her duffel bag one more time, taking each item out of the bag slowly and carefully. Sure enough, the tape was tucked into the side pocket. Jessica's shoulders sagged with relief.

When she returned to the field, Coach Laufeld was wearing her patented stern-yet-amused expression. She glanced at her watch. "Is there a problem, Jessica?"

"No. I'm ready," Jessica promised. She bent and put her tape into the boom box that was sitting on the grass. She could sense all the eyes that were on her, but she refused to glance toward the bleachers. She positioned herself on the field and raised her arms over her head.

The music started, but the opening notes of the song sounded different. Had she rewound the tape wrong? Confused, Jessica waited numbly for another few seconds.

Slowly a sinking realization penetrated Jessica's heart. It wasn't the right song. In spite of the sun blazing overhead, the sweat prickling on her neck felt cold.

She hesitated one more excruciating moment, then launched awkwardly into her routine. She tried to count the beats in her head, but the music was useless—an unrecognizable stop-and-start dance remix with a rhythm and tempo that didn't fit with her routine at all.

Jessica did her kick but missed the turn. She got so flustered, she couldn't remember what came next. She tried desperately to concentrate on her routine, but her mind kept struggling to process what had gone wrong. How could she have grabbed the wrong tape? She'd thrown it into her bag this afternoon at lunch and hadn't touched it since.

Jessica blinked back the frustrated tears that blurred her vision as all her triumphant confidence evaporated. Her movements were jerky and awkward. The tears were about to spill over.

Her routine came to a listless end as the music played on. Jessica found herself staring out at the sea of faces in the bleachers. Lila looked horrified. Cherie had both hands over her mouth and was shaking with laughter. Tia just looked shocked. But Melissa sat perfectly still with her hands in her lap, her expression a pure blank. Like she was trying hard not to give anything away.

Could it be? Could Melissa actually have done this to her?

Without waiting for the coach's comments, Jessica bolted off the field. Back in the locker room, she sank to the floor and burst into tears. Her mind flooded with all the realizations she'd been too numb to process out on the field.

Humiliation consumed her. How could anyone be so mean? So totally, blatantly evil? Jessica hadn't done anything to deserve this kind of treatment.

Cheerleading was all she had left. And now there was no way she was going to make the squad. Her already depressing life was about to become completely empty.

Will Simmons

The first night after the earthquake, my parents invited the Foxes to stay over at our house because their whole place was flooded. Melissa and her sister were supposed to sleep on the pullout couch, but Liss snuck up to my room after everyone was asleep.

We didn't even do anything. Fooling around was the last thing on either of our minds. (Yes, even mine.) I just held her while she cried, and after a while she fell asleep in my arms. I couldn't sleep, though, because she was holding on to me so tight, gripping handfuls of my T-shirt like she was clutching a life preserver. Every time I tried to move or turn, she'd squeeze tighter and kind of moan. So I just lay there and watched her sleep.

She looked so small and vulnerable, wearing an old pair of my pajamas that she was practically swimming in. I stared at her slender little hands latching like claws onto me, and I thought about how fragile she was. I wondered what the shock of the earthquake would do to her. I knew then, like I knew back in eighth grade when all her problems started, that she needed me—that she might fall apart without me. I knew, in such a deep-down way that I didn't even need to spell it out to myself. I could never leave her.

That's why it scares me to see what she's doing to Jessica. It's like she sees all the lies and manipulations as a way to get back what she had before the quake. In a weird way, it's actually making her stronger. But it's a creepy kind of strength, one that feeds off other people's weakness.

I really do care about Jessica, and it kills me that I can't do or say anything to protect her or even warn her. But I just keep thinking about the night of the quake, picturing Melissa's hands clinging to me. . . .

And I don't even want to know what she'd be capable of if she thought she might lose me.

CHAPTER
SABOTAGE
10

Tia cast a sideways glance at Melissa and shook her head in disgust as Jessica fled the field. Granted, she couldn't say for sure exactly what had happened. But for someone who had grown up with Melissa, that impassive poker face spoke volumes.

She gathered up her things and cut around to the back of the bleachers. What was Melissa's problem? She was such an incredible bitch. Jessica hadn't had the slightest idea that Will had a girlfriend when she went out with him. Not that Melissa would ever show a shred of reason or anything. It had never been her style.

Tia frowned to herself as she walked along the sideline. She was pretty sure her tryout had gone well, but even after all her hard work, she couldn't seem to concentrate on that. For some reason, the thought of Melissa sabotaging Jessica was totally bringing her down. It was disturbing to think that a girl would cling so desperately to a guy that she overlooked *his* cheating and punished a basically innocent girl instead. She hated the thought of someone being so blind to reality, holding on to a fantasy, at someone else's expense.

But it was more disturbing to realize that she could totally understand how Melissa felt.

As she entered the air-conditioned school building, Tia hugged her arms to her chest. What if it were Angel who had met some cute blond girl and trashed their three-year relationship in one night? There were going to be tons of attractive, intelligent, mature women at college. And even if Tia *wanted* to keep a choke hold on him, like Melissa was doing to Will, she couldn't keep tabs on him 24/7.

Everyone she knew seemed to see Angel as an extension of her being. Even Elizabeth, who'd just met them, laughed at the idea that Tia might leave Angel. But it really didn't matter that all her friends and her family thought he was perfect for her. Or even that *she* thought Angel was great and wonderful and adorable. None of that changed the fact that Angel was about to move on and leave her behind.

No one else could understand what it would be like to feel so far away from him—to have utterly no control over the situation. She couldn't live with herself if the stress of a long-distance relationship turned her into someone like Melissa—clinging to the past, incapable of accepting reality, unable to stand on her own.

She couldn't handle the thought of Angel calling and telling her that he had met someone else.

Or worse, finding out through the grapevine.

So this was it. She'd postponed the inevitable long enough. Tonight she would take Angel out to dinner. She'd wait in the locker room until Coach Laufeld posted the squad list. Then if she hurried, she could run home, shower, change into something drop-dead gorgeous, and be at Angel's house by the time he got off work.

Tia wanted this night to be unforgettable. Because tonight she was going to tell him it was over. She was going to set them both free. It was the right thing to do.

The lobby of Sweet Valley High was lined with large glass trophy cases. Inside, a seemingly endless line of miniature gold people balanced precariously on their stands, frozen in the act of lofting tennis rackets or crouching with footballs.

Jessica was numb as she stood gazing into the cases. The jock world of athletes and cheerleaders and games and trophies and parties had always been her scene. Now that world was closed to her. She existed outside the charmed circle of the SVH elite.

Last year, when she'd been captain of the cheerleading squad and going out with Ken Matthews, the captain of the football team, they'd been the stars of every party, dance, and beach bonfire. Now Ken was just some guy who had blown off the team, ditched half his classes, and looked like he slept in his clothes. And Jessica was a complete social reject.

Jessica sighed and glanced at the clock in the lobby. Why had she even bothered to show up here? Lila had left early to get ready for some charity event at the country club, but all the other hopefuls were gathered around the bulletin board, chattering anxiously, waiting for Coach Laufeld to post the tryout results. Jessica was standing off by herself. She wasn't exactly eager to see her failure spelled out in writing.

Jessica longed to be part of the excited crowd of girls. But thanks to Melissa, she had less chance of making the cheerleading squad than she did of being picked as the next Lord of the Dance.

"Okay, people, settle down." Coach made eye contact with almost everyone as she walked into the room, keeping her face void of expression. "I want to thank everybody who didn't make it for all your hard work at practice. Hope to see you again next year. And for those of you who did make it, probation period's not over yet. We're not going to be choosing a squad captain until after the first pep rally. I want to see how you all work together. Making captain is about leadership and teamwork, not showing off."

Teamwork. That was rich. Jessica had already proven her lack of skills in the networking department.

"Okay, enough suspense." Coach Laufeld turned to thumbtack the list to the cork board. The girls swarmed around it like dogs at feeding time.

Jessica hung back, watching them scream and high-five each other. A pixieish sophomore burst into tears. Melissa and Cherie were hugging each other and springing up and down. Jessica inhaled deeply. Did she really have the nerve to venture over there?

Suddenly she felt a hand on her shoulder and spun around, startled. Coach Laufeld was standing beside her. She didn't look happy.

"Let me put you out of your misery, Wakefield," the coach said. "You are on that list. But only because I know you're better than what I saw today. Get it together, Jessica. This is the last time I'll be cutting you any slack. Do I make myself clear?"

"Yes!" Jessica exclaimed, feeling a dumb grin spread across her face. She clasped her hands together. "I swear you won't be disappointed. Thank you sooo much!"

Coach Laufeld's face softened into a smile. "You're welcome. See you at practice." She clapped Jessica affectionately on the shoulder before walking away.

Jessica knew she was taking giddy to the extreme, but she didn't care. Coach had given her the benefit of the doubt. And she had managed to salvage a scrap of her old life.

"Can I have everybody's attention, please?" Melissa's voice was somehow demure and imperious at once. Immediately the congregation of cheerleaders stopped jumping around and fell into a hushed silence. "I think we should all get together at the Riot later for some serious celebrating. We'll get the guys from the football team to come. Sound good?"

A loud cheer went up, echoing through the lobby. Jessica gathered up her bag and headed out the door. Nothing would burst her happy bubble like having her face rubbed in Melissa's "bonding" plans.

As she passed Melissa, Jessica stared straight at her and saw a face that was triumphant . . . and slightly apprehensive. Melissa was watching her closely. Obviously she hadn't counted on sharing the squad with Jessica.

A new and intriguing thought formed in Jessica's mind as she jogged down the front steps of SVH. Maybe Elizabeth was right. If Jessica apologized to Melissa for slamming her in front of her friends—if she gave Melissa that one victory— maybe she could crawl out of this hole she was in and get on with her life.

Jessica sighed deeply as she crossed the parking lot. Making nice with Melissa would be humiliating, but it would be like pulling off a Band-Aid. She could handle one clean blow to her pride if it meant the whispering and laughing behind her back would stop. If Jessica could just get over herself long enough to make peace with Satan's most popular minion, maybe she could make a fresh start on her senior year.

Tia strode across the parking lot with her head bowed, like a condemned prisoner en route to the chair. That was what the prospect of breaking up with Angel felt like—a death sentence. But then, she reminded herself, so did four years of solitary confinement while he was at Stanford.

As she approached her parents' station wagon, she rummaged through her bag for her car keys and did a quick check in the side mirror. She was totally disheveled. A shower was definitely in order.

Tia opened the car door, blinking back a tear. She had to hold it together, or she wouldn't be able to pull off her memorable romantic evening. It was just so hard to conceive of losing Angel, when he was constantly in her thoughts.

"Hey, baby."

Tia whirled around. "Angel! What are you doing here?" She narrowed her eyes, taking in his silk dress shirt, the bouquet of orange hibiscus flowers (her favorite), and the two envelopes (one white, one yellow) he was holding. "What are you all dressed up for?"

"Picking you up." With a sly smile he placed the bouquet in her hands and kissed her on the cheek. "My dad let me off work early so I could

take you out for a celebratory dinner. Or a conso-
latory dinner. So which one is it?"

She was so thrown by the fact that *he* was here to
take *her* out that it took a second to comprehend
what he meant. "Oh . . . I made it. I'm on the squad."

"Congratulations!" He swept her into a hug
that lifted her feet an inch off the ground. "So how
come you don't seem excited?" he asked when he
let her go.

"I am—I'm just . . ." High-school activities seemed
unimportant in the face of pulling the plug on the
love of her life. "I *am* excited," she said lamely, staring
down at the armful of gloriously blazing flowers. In
fact, she wanted to die. God, he was a sweetheart.

"Okay, well, you get this one, then." Angel
handed her the yellow envelope with a flourish.

Tia tore it open and slid out a card printed
with a beautiful illustration of a gold star. Inside
Angel had written:

*Congratulations, baby!!! I knew you
could do it. I'm so proud of you, and
I know you'll have a great year.*

All my love,

Angel

Tia ignored the lump in her throat and the surge of affection swelling her rib cage. She had to be strong. "So what does the other one say? It better not be, 'I knew you *couldn't* do it.'"

"Here, see for yourself." Angel gave her the white envelope. The front of the card was a black-and-white photograph of a boy and girl holding hands. Inside it read:

All I can say is, at least now you have more free time to spend with me.

Love always,

Angel

Tears brimmed in Tia's eyes. She stared up at Angel. He was grinning like a kid who'd just won the Little League championship, his brown eyes shining. Her heart felt like it was teetering on a cliff. How could she break his heart just to cover herself? She was ready to give up, and he was promising love always.

A tear snaked down her cheek. Tia gave up the fight. She threw her arms around Angel and wept noisily into his chest.

"Don't cry!" Angel's voice was soothing and amused at once. "Tia, what's wrong?"

"Nothing," Tia sobbed. For the moment at least, it was the truth. Her eyeliner was probably streaming down her face, but it didn't matter. She knew now that there was no way she could give Angel up. And even though she was sure the next few months would be hard, her heart felt lighter than it had in days.

She lifted her face and gazed at him, cherishing the fact that he was hers. And he would be forever. "You're just so sweet, it's almost sickening. Of course I'll always have time for you." They smiled their smile at each other.

"C'mon," he said. "Let's hit the town."

"You're kidding." Tia sniffled. "I have to go home and shower first." She laughed through her tears. "I'm a total mess."

Angel chuckled. He wove his fingers through her hair, cradling the side of her head in his palm. "You look beautiful."

"Thanks, baby."

As Angel leaned over to hug her, Tia caught a glimpse of her tear-streaked face, half-fallen ponytail, and blotchy skin in the car window and smiled. At that moment she actually felt beautiful.

"Hi, Mrs. Sandborn! Hey, Megan!" Elizabeth called out as she entered the kitchen. "You look nice," she told Mrs. Sandborn, sizing up her black evening dress and heeled shoes. "Are you going out somewhere?"

"Thank you, Elizabeth," Mrs. Sandborn said as she placed her wallet into her pocketbook and snapped it closed. "I'm going out with a friend."

Megan turned away from the refrigerator and smiled. "Hey, Liz. How was your shift?"

Elizabeth groaned and lowered herself into a chair at the kitchen table. "Hellish. We're always mobbed on Friday night. Plus the espresso machine sprayed all over me, so I reek of coffee." She eased one foot out of her sandal and massaged her arches. "I swear, I'm getting too old for this."

Mrs. Sandborn laughed loudly. "Never ever say that around a graying old woman," she said.

"You're not graying," Elizabeth protested.

"Thanks to Clairol," Mrs. Sandborn answered, pulling her fingers through her hair with a flourish. She laughed again and planted a kiss on top of Megan's head. "I'll see you later, sweetie. Bye, Elizabeth."

"Have fun, Mom," Megan said. "Don't do anything I wouldn't do."

"Don't count on it!" Mrs. Sandborn called.

Megan cringed and looked at Elizabeth. "Hot date," she explained.

"Enough said," Elizabeth answered, sensing that the subject was better left alone.

Megan set down a jar of mayonnaise on the kitchen counter. "Do you want a sandwich?"

"No, thanks," Elizabeth said, leaning back and

146

patting her stomach. "I was scarfing biscotti all through my shift. I feel like a blimp."

"Right. You're like a stick." Megan took out a head of lettuce and a jar of mustard and kicked the refrigerator door shut. "I wish I had your body."

"Well, if you had my body, every single one of your muscles would be aching right now," Elizabeth pointed out. She folded her arms on the table and rested her head on her elbow. "Hey, I'm sorry about leaving the *Oracle* meeting early. I had to run home and change before work. Did I miss anything?"

"Not really." Megan was spreading mustard on a piece of pita bread. "We just brainstormed some ideas for expanding sports coverage."

"Gee, I'm so sorry I missed that," Elizabeth said dryly. "We really don't do enough to glorify jocks at SVH."

Megan turned toward Elizabeth and laughed, flashing her braces. "At my old school the day they announced we might have discovered a cure for cancer, the big news around ECH was that our basketball team beat Big Mesa in the play-offs."

"Unreal." Elizabeth chuckled.

"Mr. Collins wasn't too psyched about you leaving, though," Megan said tentatively.

"Really?" Elizabeth said. "I guess twice in one week is a bit much."

"Well, you only missed, like, ten minutes this time," Megan said. "I think if you just talked to him about it, he'd be cool. When I told him I'd have to be coming and going until soccer season was over, he said he was glad to see I was so involved."

"Yeah. He'll understand," Elizabeth agreed. "Mr. Collins is a good guy."

"And he's cute too," Megan said, her eyes bright. "For a teacher."

Elizabeth smiled. In spite of her exhaustion, she felt a faint glow of contentment watching Megan putter around in the kitchen. Megan was so earnest about the paper, she again reminded Elizabeth of herself . . . well, herself at Megan's age, really. Elizabeth had even had a crush on Mr. Collins once herself. If she had to be away from home and her parents and particularly from Jessica, at least it was nice to be living with someone who felt a little like family.

"Okay, I think I may have recovered sufficiently to get myself some juice." Elizabeth yawned, lifting her head.

"Oh, I finished it." Megan turned back to her sandwich. "But there's another bottle in the pantry."

"Thanks." Elizabeth got up and shuffled across the kitchen on her angry feet.

As she passed the doorway to the living room, a flash of movement caught her eye. When she saw what it was, she stopped dead.

On the living-room couch Conner and Maria were locked in a furious tangle of limbs, their faces

148

welded together in passionate kiss. Elizabeth gripped the door frame in surprise. She looked away quickly, but her eyes were drawn back against her will.

Conner cupped Maria's face in his hands, drawing her still closer to him, and Maria let out a blissful little murmur. That one sound curdled Elizabeth's blood more than any scream ever could.

"Liz?"

Elizabeth nearly jumped out of her skin at the sound of Megan's voice at her side. Conner's eyes opened, and he looked right at Elizabeth. She was snagged. There was no way he could have misread her horrified face. But then his eyes squeezed shut again. He couldn't have seen her. He would have broken apart from Maria, and they were still going at it full force.

I can't take this, Elizabeth thought. She pulled Megan out of the doorway, but not before Megan noticed the cause of Elizabeth's sheet-white complexion. When she looked back at Elizabeth, her eyes were wide.

Perfect. That just capped everything off. Megan looked up to her, and now she was standing here watching Elizabeth lose it over her big brother. Panicked, Elizabeth turned away quickly and swallowed the mass choking her throat, fighting to control her face.

"You know what?" Elizabeth said, forcing a smile. "I have a sudden craving for a hamburger and fries. Let's go to First and Ten. My treat." She grabbed Megan's wrist.

"But I thought you weren't hungry," Megan protested.

"Biscotti doesn't stick with you," Elizabeth said, snatching her keys from the counter.

"But my sandwich!" Megan said as she was pulled out the door.

"Don't worry about it," Elizabeth said. They'd deal with the cleanup later. All Elizabeth could think about right now was getting as far away from Maria's blissful little sighs as quickly as possible.

<u>Essay</u> <u>2:</u> Describe an experience that had a significant effect on your life or profoundly changed your belief system and/or perspective. (200 words or less)

Okay, I know how I <u>shouldn</u>t answer this question. I know that the exact response an Ivy League school <u>doesn</u>t want to hear is, "Well, I met this amazing guy, and he totally changed my life." But I cant help it. I sit down to write, and all I can think about is Conner, Conner, Conner. I just want to regress back to seventh grade and write our names together in big, loopy hearts all over my notebook.

The fact is, Conner has profoundly changed my perspective on life. See, Ive always been a realist. I never believed in love at first sight. I thought relationships were something you worked on over time, just like grades.

But that doesnt even begin to explain the way

Conner dropped into my life from out of the blue. I've never experienced the kind of feelings I have for him and definitely not this fast. He's made me realize there's more to life than studying and working and taking myself really seriously all the time.

And even more than that, he's changed my perspective on myself. Just the fact that he's with me makes me feel like there must be something special about me.

Granted, I get good grades, I have friends, and I know I'm not Quasimodo or anything, but I've never really thought of myself as smart or cool or beautiful or whatever.

But when I'm with Conner, it's different. Just one smile from him, and all my petty little worries about school and work and applications fade away, and I feel like I'm floating on air. I know none of that stuff Liz said about him could actually be true. The way he looks at me, the way he talks to me, the way he touches me . . . I don't believe for a second he could just be playing me.

Then again, I almost hope what Liz said is
true or that it was true until he met me. It just
makes what we have that much more special to
think that he s never felt that way before about
anyone. Maybe I really have changed him . . .
just like he s changed me.

Elizabeth wadded up a Kleenex and tossed it at the wastebasket on the other side of the room. It teetered for a moment on the rim, then skittered to the floor. Exhaling in exasperation, she fell back against the pillows. Even gravity was conspiring against her.

She dragged herself up from the bed and threw the tissue ball away. As she stumbled back across the room, more tears blurred her sight. Visions of Maria and Conner together, kissing passionately, holding each other, laughing over some stupid secret, swam before her eyes. She felt weak, drained, and horribly betrayed.

Which made no sense, of course. Conner wasn't hers and never had been. And Maria didn't even know Elizabeth liked him.

"But I *don't* like him. I don't," she told herself. She walked up to the mirror that hung over her dresser and stared fiercely at her haggard reflection. "How can I like someone so obnoxious, unfeeling, immature, closed off, and completely

154

self-centered?" Elizabeth lifted her chin and stood still for a moment, letting her words hang in the air. Then she burst into tears all over again.

In spite of her better judgment, in spite of all signs to the contrary, Elizabeth had allowed herself to hope that one day she would be in Conner's arms. They would share a deep connection that went beyond their superficial differences. It was crushing to know that Maria was living her dream.

Elizabeth realized she was shivering. She crawled into bed and burrowed under the blankets. She didn't remember feeling so torn apart when she broke up with Todd, and that had been a real relationship, not an infatuation.

She pulled the covers up to her chin. It would be so nice to be at home in her bedroom on Calico Drive, with Jessica just on the other side of the wall, banging around and singing along with the stereo at the top of her lungs. She missed her twin, she missed her parents, and she missed the feeling—which she'd taken for granted when she had it—of being safe and sound where she belonged.

Wearily Elizabeth closed her aching eyes. For a second she considered calling Jessica and spilling the whole absurd story of her crush on Conner. But admitting it out loud would make it too real. And she didn't want to make it real. She wanted to make it go away.

Elizabeth took a deep breath and wiped her

eyes on her sleeve. She couldn't afford to lose any more of her dignity. She reached for the phone on her nightstand and dialed a number she knew by heart.

Enid answered on the second ring.

"Oh, hey, Liz, what's up?" Her voice was animated, almost giddy. Without waiting for Elizabeth to respond, she went on, "I had the *best* night. Ileana and I went over to Judith's house and had a *Xena* marathon. Judith has, like, *every* episode on tape. Then we went on-line and hung out in this chat room with these really cute guys. I mean, they *sounded* like really cute guys." Enid giggled.

Elizabeth wondered if Enid's voice had always sounded so shrill when she was excited. It felt like ages since they'd talked.

"That sounds like fun," Elizabeth said with strained politeness. "Listen, Enid, I kind of need to talk to you about something."

"Oh my God, Liz, you sound terrible!" Enid's voice snapped into concerned mode. "What's wrong?"

Elizabeth exhaled shakily. She used to talk to Enid every day, but now that they had new friends and new lives, it was hard to know where to start. Elizabeth decided to just jump into the deep end.

"Enid, I need a place to stay." There was a long pause on the other end of the line.

"What do you mean? Did you and Megan have a fight?" Enid said finally.

"No, no, Megan's great. It's her brother, Conner."
Her voice broke on his name.

"*Conner?*" Enid squealed. "Cute Conner, from
our writing class?"

"Yeah. I mean, no! He's not cute. He's a total
jerk," Elizabeth blurted. "He's making my life hell."

Elizabeth tried to ignore the pain in her heart
caused by her own words. "Anyway, Enid, I was
wondering if I could crash with you for a little
while." Elizabeth crossed her fingers.

Another pause. Elizabeth had to fill the silence
before Enid said no.

"I know it's a lot to ask, but I swear, you'd
hardly even notice I was there."

"Okay, I'll ask," Enid said slowly. "It'll probably
be cool, but just so you know, there's a chance my
parents won't go for it. Things have been kind of
tight for us since the quake. Hey, what about asking Maria? Her house is a lot bigger than ours."

Elizabeth winced. "Her parents vetoed it," she lied.

"My parents went to bed already, but I'll try to
catch them in the morning," Enid said, sounding
like she wasn't sure she meant it. "Me and Ileana
are meeting at House of Java, if you want to stop
by and find out what they said."

"Actually, I have a shift tomorrow, so I'll probably see you there." It was odd to think of meeting
up with Enid and her new friends.

"Okay, cool. See you then."

"Bye, Enid. And thanks." Elizabeth hung up the phone, got up, and rummaged through her dresser. In moments she had pulled on her favorite flannel pajamas and was curled up under the covers again. It felt good to have taken some action. Action was good.

Everything was practically settled now. She would go stay at Enid's. They'd catch up, and it would be like old times again. And most importantly, she would never have to deal with Conner again.

She wondered why she didn't feel relieved.

"You should go," Conner said in a regretful voice, pulling away from Maria. "I have a guitar lesson tomorrow, and I need to practice."

Maria encircled his waist with both arms and squeezed tightly. Her lips looked puffy from kissing, and Conner thought she looked even more beautiful than usual. Too bad.

"What if I don't want to go?" she asked, raising her eyebrows.

"Don't make me use my secret weapon," Conner said. "You should never have let me find out that you're ticklish."

"Okay! Okay, I give." Maria pulled back, but it didn't last long. She kept her eyes on his face and slowly slid her hand down his back, sending chills up his spine. Conner gave in. He slipped his fingers under the hem of her shirt and teasingly worked his hands up her back.

In another instant her mouth was upon him, forceful but soft and yielding at once. Conner closed his eyes, enjoying the kiss. Why fight a good thing?

Suddenly the stricken, deathly pale face of Elizabeth Wakefield loomed before him.

Conner's eyes flew open in alarm. He disengaged, gasping for breath. Maria's eyes fluttered open, and her moist lips curled into a languid smile.

His gaze lingered on Maria's sleepy-lidded eyes, the lush curled fringe of her lashes. She really was strikingly beautiful. Not the kind of girl who made you fantasize about someone else.

So why couldn't he get Elizabeth's face—that *look* on her face—out of his head?

"You okay, Conner?" Maria asked softly.

"Of course." To prove it, he leaned in to kiss her again.

Conner liked being with Maria. She was a pretty cool girl, and one of the top five kissers he'd had the pleasure of kissing. Plus he got the sense that she wasn't all that experienced with guys. He loved sensing her hesitation at every turn, then feeling her let herself go completely.

But maybe it had been a mistake to let Maria come over. She seemed to take it as a sign that they were a couple, and that definitely was not Conner's intention. Then, of course, there was Elizabeth. . . .

But so what if she saw them kissing? They were all adults. Why did he feel like he'd been caught cheating or something?

Maybe he had *wanted* Elizabeth to see him with Maria just to get under her skin. But that was stupid. He didn't have anything to prove to Elizabeth.

Conner wasn't aware that he had broken apart from Maria until he heard her voice.

"Conner," she breathed, barely audible. Her chin was tilted back, her eyes half shut. "Do you really want me to leave?"

"I have things to do, Maria," he said as he pulled his hands out from under her shirt. Maria's eyes flew open and she sat up straight. For a second the expression on her face was pure disappointment.

He smiled faintly. He knew Maria wanted to stay, but there wasn't really any point. His mind was obviously on other . . . things.

"Okay. I've got a lot to do too," Maria said. Her hands fumbled with the top two buttons of her blouse, which Conner had unbuttoned at some point. She stood up, a little shakily, and picked up her crocheted bag from the floor. "Okay, so . . . call me tomorrow?" she asked, her voice expectant.

Conner shrugged noncommittally. "I'll talk to you," he said. Why did they all feel the need to say stuff like "call me"? Couldn't they chill and be happy just hanging out and making out?

Maria leaned over to give him one last light kiss

on the lips. "Bye," she said in a small, almost shy voice.

"Later," Conner said lightly. He was getting a little antsy. Maria's doe eyes were still trained on him, like she was waiting for some kind of assurance.

After a second she shrugged awkwardly and turned to leave. Conner listened for the sound of the front door closing, then let out a sigh of relief.

Maria was cool, but she was already starting to get high maintenance. Girls could be so clingy. *Give her a chance,* Conner's conscience told him. *You've only known her for twenty-four hours.*

Conner dropped onto the sofa, grabbed a magazine, and flipped through it absently, snapping the pages.

Fine. Maria getting possessive he could handle. But Elizabeth staring at him like he was a devil-worshiping serial killer, just because he happened to be hanging out with one of her friends, was more than Conner wanted to deal with. If there was one thing he hated, it was drama. And now he'd somehow managed to bring a whole lot of drama home with him.

He stood abruptly and grabbed his jacket. There were too many women in this house. Women with problems and expectations. He needed to be somewhere that wasn't here. He had to find some guys, score a few beers, and mellow out in a place where there was no talking, no thinking, and especially no drama.

*   *   *

Jessica took a deep breath and ran through one final mental rehearsal.

Listen, Melissa, I know you hate me, but I swear I didn't know that Will had a girlfriend—or that you were her. Now that we're both on the squad, can't we just put all this behind us and be civil to each other?

Oh, who was she kidding? She was a lamb headed for the slaughter. As Jessica threaded her way through the crowd at the Riot, every strobelight flash was like a pin to her eye. She'd told Lila she wasn't going in case she lost her nerve, but now she wished she weren't walking in alone. She felt so conspicuous. And her hands had become the state's leading producer of sweat.

Jessica nervously smoothed down the skirt of her dress. She'd taken pains to select just the right outfit—something that exuded innocence without making her look wimpy. Finally she'd settled on a white sundress embroidered with delicate baby-blue flowers. She still didn't feel the slightest bit confident, but at least she didn't look like a loser.

As she reached the back of the room, Jessica spotted them. Most of the new cheerleading squad, along with several of the jocks from the football team, was assembled at a large, round table. Her eyes found Melissa instantly.

Her hair was pulled back, making her chin and cheekbones look sharp. As usual she was sitting between Gina and Cherie, her hands folded primly on the table as if she were running a board meeting. Lila and Amy sat on the other side of Cherie. Jessica didn't see Tia anywhere, but all the other ECH cheerleaders were present. There was only one empty seat, between Annie Whitman and a football player Jessica didn't recognize.

As she approached the table, conversation ceased. Jessica swallowed hard. In spite of the music blasting, she felt like every step she made, every hammering beat of her heart, was acutely audible. She followed their eyes following her as she pulled back the chair and lowered herself into it.

Melissa stared down at the table with an emotionless see-no-evil, hear-no-evil expression.

Jessica felt her throat closing up, but she opened her mouth to speak. "Listen, I—"

Cherie turned darkly glittering eyes on her. "What do you think you're doing?" It was more of an accusation than a question.

Jessica's mouth dropped open. Her apology was strangled in her throat. Everyone at the table was staring at her, smirking—everyone except Lila, Annie, and Amy. They were staring down at the table, looking as pained as Jessica felt. And Melissa's impassive gaze was still fixed on her hands.

"No one invited you," Gina added. Then she turned her face toward Melissa and muttered, "Slut."

Melissa's mouth twisted into a quick smile, but she squelched it fast.

"What?" Jessica gasped.

Gina looked up. "Oh, nothing," she said.

Jessica felt her hands start to shake. This was so unfair. She was trying to take the high road, trying to be mature. But it didn't matter. Nothing she did would ever make a difference. Jessica pushed herself out of the chair on weak knees. She couldn't take it anymore.

"Fine. Don't listen to me," she said, staring at Melissa's lowered eyes. The girl didn't even have the guts to look Jessica in the face. "I don't need this, and I don't need any of you." She didn't need to be part of this back-stabbing little crowd. El Carro meant nothing to her last year, and it meant nothing to her now.

Then she looked at Lila and Amy.

"Come on, you guys, let's get out of here," she said, managing to keep her voice remarkably even.

Nobody moved.

Lila and Amy glanced at each other, then focused on the floor. Cherie snickered into her hands.

"She still doesn't get it, does she?" Gina laughed softly and shook her head, as if she couldn't believe Jessica's naivete. Jessica's blood ran cold as the full force of the realization hit her.

This wasn't happening. This couldn't be happening. She felt her lips begin to tremble and fought hard to keep her face blank. *They're not coming with you*, a strangely calm voice warned her. *Just walk away. You have no friends.*

Choking back a sob, Jessica turned and headed for the door. Melissa and Will had won. They'd taken away her school, they'd taken away her reputation, and now, somehow, they'd taken away her friends.

As she pushed her way blindly through the crowd, Jessica heard a voice behind her. "Jessica, wait!"

She spun around, ready to throw desperate, grateful arms around whoever was still willing to stick by her. But she froze when she saw that it was Will, undoubtedly sent to pour salt on her fresh, open wound.

Frantic, Jessica stumbled as fast as she could toward the exit. Will's voice echoed behind her for an agonizing moment before it was swallowed up by the noise of the Riot.

Please just leave me alone! Her only remaining hope was to preserve the last pitiful shreds of dignity she had left by managing to get out of the Riot without letting them see her cry.

melissa Fox

One of the worst things about the earthquake was having to ditch my summer plans and go stay at my freaky aunt's apartment in Baltimore. My aunt has <u>mice</u>. Not cute little Disney mice, but big, ugly gray rodents. I was always finding droppings in the kitchen. It was <u>so</u> disgusting. And all over the apartment were those glue traps. You know, those boards where they get stuck and I guess eventually just starve to death. You don't have to be one of those crunchy, cruelty-free-products people to think those traps are nauseatingly inhumane.

Anyway, one day I was alone

in the apartment and I heard this anguished squeaking, and I knew a mouse had gotten caught in one. I tiptoed into the kitchen. There was this little gray thing, stuck, its legs scrambling in the air. I've never felt so sick to my stomach in my whole life.

I couldn't stand hearing it cry, so I got the broom and dustpan like I'd seen my aunt do before. My hands were shaking so hard. When I got up close, I saw its little eyes look up at me, and I lost it.

It freaked me out to see something so helpless. And I had to kill it. There was nothing else I could do. But I hated it for being a defenseless little

creature and for making me
hate myself for getting rid
of it.

I'd rather deal with something
that could fight back. Then I
wouldn't feel so evil.

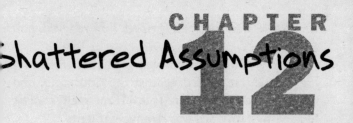
Shadows flitted across the ceiling, warping into faces, stretching into limbs that twined around and around each other like vines. Elizabeth blinked rapidly, unsure whether her eyes had been open or closed, whether she was awake or dreaming. After calling Enid, she'd managed to drift into a fitful half sleep, where nightmare images melted imperceptibly into wakeful thoughts. She'd be exhausted in the morning for sure.

Elizabeth lifted her heavy head and kneaded her pillow, then settled back down and closed her eyes. The shadows crept forward again, closing in on her. Then a slow creaking noise split the silence like a bolt of light. A dark figure loomed before her.

Elizabeth sat up straight. Her door was open, illuminating her room with a wedge-shaped beam of light. A tall figure was silhouetted in the doorway. Elizabeth was about to start fumbling for some kind of blunt object to use as a weapon when her eyes adjusted to the light, and she realized it was Conner.

"You scared me!" she gasped, half relieved, half annoyed.

"Sorry," Conner mumbled softly. He was swaying a little. He leaned against the doorjamb, and his eyes searched her face. "I'm really sorry, Elizabeth." His voice was strangely intent.

Silence hung thick in the air. "Did you want something?" Elizabeth asked after a minute. She realized she was clutching her blankets but couldn't make her fingers relax their grip.

Conner took a step toward her, then another. As he came closer, she could see that his eyes were rimmed with red and full of sorrow. He looked *so* sad and . . . scared. He pushed his hands through his hair.

"For everything," he said. He had to be drunk. Elizabeth's pulse pounded in her ears. Not surprising, since her heart was in her mouth.

He was just inches from her bed now. She could feel his warmth—hear his breath. Elizabeth knew she should kick him out or leave the room herself, but she was entranced. Conner stepped into a shadow, and all she could make out was his profile—the gentle incline of his nose, the curves of his lips. There was no sound. They were both holding their breath now.

Conner leaned toward her. He was going to kiss her. Elizabeth closed her eyes as her heart brimmed with anticipation. Then Elizabeth smelled his sour breath, and in that instant fear won out. Involuntarily she shrank back against the wall.

"Conner—," she said, her voice like a shot in the shadowed stillness of the room.

Conner straightened up and a cloud of confusion crossed his face. Then he chuckled softly. He put his palms up in a gesture of surrender and took a step back.

Elizabeth had never felt so stupid in her entire life.

Wait! Don't go! she thought as he turned and retreated toward the door. She stared at the outline of his broad shoulders, regret and longing and confusion churning within her.

"Conner," she said again. Her voice was a near whisper, but he paused in the doorway and slowly turned around.

In the light from the hall Elizabeth saw his eyebrows arch provocatively and his lips stretch into a seductive smile.

"By the way, Wakefield," he said in a low voice, "I have to say, you even make flannel sexy."

As soon as she emerged from the Riot, Jessica unleashed the knot of sobs that was lodged in her throat like a stone. She lurched numbly across the parking lot, her vision clouded by the tears spilling violently down her cheeks. The night was warm, but the cool breeze whipped cold on her wet face.

How could her friends do this to her?

Reaching the Jeep, she leaned against the driver's-side door, momentarily unable to move. Crowds of people rushed around her, laughing, whispering, having fun. She'd never felt so desperately, helplessly alone.

Everyone she trusted, everyone she counted on, had deserted her when she needed them most. What had Melissa done to make them reject her like that?

Jessica heard a car pull in nearby. She lifted her tear-streaked face and saw Todd Wilkins, Elizabeth's ex-boyfriend, getting out of his BMW.

Jessica sucked in her breath and hastily wiped her eyes. She couldn't remember ever being so glad to see Todd. In all honesty, she'd never been his biggest fan, but now Todd's open, kind face was a welcome reminder of her stable, predictable, preearthquake life. If anyone would give Jessica a straight answer about what was going on, Todd would.

Todd bent over to lock his car. His brown hair hung down, obscuring his face. When he looked up and saw her, he glanced around nervously as if he was searching for an escape route. No shocker there. She must have looked completely hysterical.

Todd stuffed both hands into his jacket pockets and stood as if at attention.

"Jess," he said tentatively.

"Todd, I'm so glad to see you," Jessica gasped

breathlessly. She laid an imploring hand on the sleeve of his varsity jacket. "Do you know what's going on . . . I mean . . . with me?"

"I guess." Todd shifted his weight.

"You know about all the names they're calling me?" In spite of her best efforts, her lower lip trembled and her eyes started to water.

Todd nodded again, his brown eyes trained on the ground.

"So, *why*, Todd? Why do Lila and Amy and everyone else suddenly hate me?"

"I don't know what's up with them," Todd said. "You know your friends aren't my favorite people."

"Then the guys, Todd. You—you must have heard Will or one of the El Carro guys say something! Why are they calling me a . . . a slut?" A sob exploded from Jessica's chest as she uttered the word.

Todd shrugged, resigned. "Well, Jess," he said in a defeated voice, "I hate to be the one to say this to your face, but what do you expect?"

Jessica stood frozen, staring dumbly at Todd.

"What do I expect?" she repeated feebly.

He took a step backward, finally meeting her eyes, his face a mix of contempt and pity. "Yeah. I mean, if you hit on one girl's boyfriend and sleep with *another* guy that same night, what do you *think* people are going to call you?"

*   *   *

The string of silver bells on the door tinkled. Elizabeth glanced up and saw a goth chick with a stuffed-panda backpack. She scanned the room. It was a standard Saturday-morning crowd. Dreadlocked dude with seashell necklace. Blond junior who'd returned from summer break with a much perkier nose than the one she had last year. House of Java was overrun with SVH students, but there was no sign of Enid.

Elizabeth tapped the counter with her fingertips as she poured cappuccino into a mug with her other hand. Was Enid talking to her mother right now? Had they already made a decision?

She wiped foam from her fingers onto her apron and glanced at her watch. It wasn't even eleven yet, and already she was getting impatient. The clatter of coffee cups and the upbeat ska music piped through the speakers threatened to fray her last nerve.

Of course, it was no shock that her mood wasn't exactly sunshine and roses. By the time Elizabeth had finally fallen asleep, her room had been gray with the bleary light of dawn. Now she was seriously considering whether she could rewire the coffee machines to hook her up with an intravenous espresso drip.

Finally the jingling bells sounded for Enid. She walked in, wearing a camouflage T-shirt and a multicolored peasant skirt and chatting with a pale girl who carried a lunch box—had to be Ileana.

"What would be even cooler is if they could just merge Ozzfest and Lilith Fair," the lunch-box girl was saying as they approached the counter.

"Hey, Enid," Elizabeth said.

Enid turned startled eyes on Elizabeth, as if she'd just noticed her standing there. "Oh, hey, Liz."

"Can I talk to you for a second?" Elizabeth asked, flicking her eyes at Enid's friend.

"I'll go get a table," Ileana said with a shrug.

"What's up?" Enid asked, hoisting herself onto a stool.

Elizabeth cleared her throat. She kept her eyes on the stream of coffee she was pouring. "Well, about what we talked about last night—"

"Oh, right," Enid interrupted, slapping her palm against her forehead. "I'm sorry, Liz, I haven't had a chance to ask yet. My mom left for work before I got up. But I promise I'll ask tonight."

Elizabeth set the coffees on the counter before Enid. She couldn't believe what she was about to do. "Actually, what I wanted to say was . . . thanks for being supportive and everything, but don't bother asking your mom. I'm going to stay with the Sandborns."

The look that crossed Enid's face was one of surprise mingled with relief. "Are you sure? What about Conner?"

Elizabeth looked down at her sandals. "Um,

he's not all that bad," she mumbled, feeling heat suffuse her face. "I was just overreacting. You were right. I should probably just try talking to him. We have to clear the air." That was the understatement of the year.

Enid shook her head. "Okay, Liz, as long as everything's cool. Are you really sure about this?"

Elizabeth met Enid's eyes. She nodded firmly. "I'm sure."

She was lying, of course. She had no idea what she was doing. She couldn't even imagine how Maria would react if she knew Elizabeth had almost jumped her new boyfriend's bones. By sticking it out at the Sandborns', Elizabeth might be making the biggest mistake of her life. Conner's every move would register on her mental radar whether she liked it or not.

But in another way, she knew exactly what she was doing, and she'd never been surer of anything in her life. For better or worse, Elizabeth was going with her heart . . . even if that meant losing her mind.

ELIZABETH WAKEFIELD
11:58 A.M.

I feel like one of those dumb coeds in B horror movies who insist on wandering, alone and scantily clad, into the dark, deserted house. Everyone in the audience is screaming, "Turn back, you idiot!" but of course she just goes ahead-and ends up getting hacked into cocktail franks by some guy in a hockey mask.

JESSICA WAKEFIELD
1:04 P.M.

I'm never getting out of bed again.

CONNER MCDERMOTT
1:07 P.M.

I have a splitting headache. And its not for the reason you think. Unlike my mother, I know when to quit. Its because I remember what I did last night.

I've never reacted well to drama, but normally its flung on me by people beyond my control.

Its a hell of a lot worse when I actually do something to perpetuate it.

MARIA SLATER

1:15 P.M.

I don t know what s wrong with Liz. Not only is she totally dissing me for these new friends, but she can t even be happy that I have someone new to hang out with too. She can t even try to see what I see in Conner to take five minutes of her precious time and give him a chance.

I guess I can t blame her, though. I didn t exactly break bread with her new crowd. And all I can think about is Conner the last time I saw him and when I can see him again.

It s so weird. Me. With a boyfriend. Wow.